P9-DNZ-254

Staci heard Matt in his room. The door was slightly ajar. She knocked, then walked in. "Matt—"

He swung around and dropped an open bottle of pills on the floor. She hardly recognized her brother's angry, red face.

"Who said you could come into my room?" he yelled at her.

"The—the door was partly open. I wasn't trying to sneak up on you." She started to pick up some of the pills.

"Don't touch those!" he shouted.

Staci backed away.

"I don't know why people can't leave me alone!"

Shocked and hurt, tears filled Staci's eyes. "Matt, I only—"

"Get out!" he screamed, gave her a push and slammed the door.

If you want to know more about steroid abuse, here are two places to call:

1-800-622-HELP.
The National Institute of Drug Abuse offers referrals for treatment and counseling, 24 hours a day.

1-800-257-7800.
The HazeldenCork Sports Education Program will provide information on steroid abuse and how to combat it.

DEAD WRONG

by Alida E. Young

*To Milly Ames, friend, mentor,
idea-giver, and critic*

*Special thanks to my son Ben and to
Wayne King, M.D., for their invaluable help.
Many thanks also to Zac Copeland and
Deputy Coroner John Quinn.*

Published by Willowisp Press
801 94th Avenue North, St. Petersburg, Florida 33702

Copyright © 1992 by Willowisp Press,
a division of PAGES, Inc.

All rights reserved. No portion of this book may be repro-
duced, stored in a retrieval system, or transmitted, in any
form or by any means, electronic, mechanical, photocopying,
recording, or otherwise without written permission from the
publisher.

Printed in the United States of America

4 6 8 10 9 7 5

ISBN 0-87406-602-6

One

STACI Malloy jumped up as her brother Matt took the handoff from the Rancho Grande quarterback. All the people around her cheered as Matt sliced through the line and broke into the open. He headed for the goal line.

"Go, Matt! Go!" she yelled.

A large player from Lincoln High tackled Matt and threw him to the ground.

"You big creep!" Staci shouted. "Pick on somebody your own size!" Matt got up slowly.

"Hey, take it easy," her friend Deneen said. "Your brother's tough. He can take it."

That was true. Staci knew that Matt spent hours pumping iron and working out. "I know," she said. "But this is a football game, not a war. That guy looks mad enough to smash a brick wall with his fists."

"He's probably a steroid geek," Rick said.

Deneen sighed. "I think he's kind of cute."

"He's an animal," Staci said, then turned to Rick. "What do you mean by steroid geek?"

"He's probably using anabolic steroids to bulk himself up, to make himself bigger, stronger, and more aggressive," Rick told her. "Lots of kids use them."

"So what's wrong with getting bigger and stronger?" Deneen asked. "I mean, football players are supposed to be big and strong, aren't they?"

Rick gave her a disgusted look. "Because steroids are dangerous. And illegal."

Rick Wagner was fifteen, a year older than Staci and Deneen, but the three had known each other since they were little kids. The Malloys, Wagners, and Cusiks sometimes spent holidays and vacations together. Even though Rick hoped to make the basketball team this year, and he did a lot of running, he wasn't a full-time jock. That was one of the things Staci liked about him—he was interested in lots of different things.

"Well, I'm glad Matt would never take drugs," Staci said. She knew her brother was against drinking beer and smoking. "He believes in taking care of his body."

Staci turned back to the game. Rancho Grande was on the 9-yard line. Matt caught

6

a screen pass and carried the ball to the 5-yard line. "I wonder if any college scouts came tonight?" she asked Rick.

"I don't think so," Rick answered. "Probably not until we play Hawthorne."

Staci knew how important the Hawthorne game was to Matt. The game would probably decide the conference championship. Plus, Matt was hoping to get a scholarship to a college. He had even talked to scouts from great schools such as UCLA, Harvard and Stanford. Matt got good grades, but Staci knew there was no way their parents could afford to send Matt to such good colleges. If Matt could play well the rest of the season, there was a great chance he'd get to go to one of the best colleges in the whole country.

With only 19 seconds left in the half, Rancho Grande lined up on the 5-yard line. The crowd yelled and stamped their feet to urge on the team. Staci could pick out her mother's voice even from a few rows away. Julie Malloy used to be a marathon runner and never missed a game. Luckily, she understood that Staci wanted to watch the game with her friends, and never sat with them.

Everyone was standing except Matt's girlfriend. Krystal Karas (she always introduced herself as "Krystal with a K") sat directly in front of Staci. Instead of watching the game, Krystal was reading something. *Some girlfriend she is,* Staci thought.

On third down, the quarterback pitched the ball to Matt, and Matt bulled his way down to the 1-yard line.

The crowd groaned. "Go for it! Go for it!" the fans yelled. Instead the coach decided to try a field goal. But the kicker missed, and the first half came to an end.

"Who wants something to eat or drink?" Rick asked.

"I could go for some popcorn," Staci said.

"You could always go for some popcorn," Deneen said, knowing Staci's weakness for popcorn. "I'll have a soda," she told Rick.

Rick collected everybody's money. Then he tapped Krystal on the shoulder. She jumped as if her mind had been a million miles away.

"Uhh, how about you, Krystal?" he asked.

Krystal looked up from her notebook. "What?" she asked, glancing around.

"Want something from the refreshment stand?" Rick asked.

"A diet soda would be fine."

As soon as Rick left, Staci leaned over and asked Krystal, "What are you reading? How come you're not watching Matt play."

Staci had tried her best to like Krystal because she was Matt's girlfriend. But it hadn't been easy, and sometimes she had to force herself to be friendly.

Krystal tossed her hair over her shoulder. "I'm trying to learn this long speech by Monday. Mrs. Owens is taping it to send to the Academy."

The Academy! It was the same school where Staci hoped to go next summer. Just like Matt wanting to earn a scholarship to college, Staci's dream was to earn a scholarship to the summer school of the Academy of Fine Arts in Los Angeles. She wanted to study creative writing. Last summer, Deneen had gotten a scholarship for music. Although it was only fall, the school was taking applications for scholarships. The waiting list was so long that they only took the best students. And only one student could apply from Rancho Grande High.

Krystal was Staci's strongest competition for next summer's session. Krystal was pretty, tall, blond, a straight-A student, and the drama coach's pet. Staci wasn't sure that she disliked Krystal because she was a bit jealous, or because Krystal had a good chance of beating her out. Or maybe because Krystal was dating Matt. Staci felt that nobody, no matter how pretty and talented, was good enough for her brother.

"Reciting a speech is a lot easier than my project," Staci said. "I have to write a 10-page story."

"Why bother?" Krystal asked. "Your English grades aren't good enough."

"How do you know?" Staci demanded.

"Matt told me."

Feeling a little betrayed by her brother, Staci sank back on the bench.

"Don't let her get to you," Deneen whispered. "You know your story counts more points than your English grade."

"She makes me mad," Staci whispered back. "She's so—so—smug. She acts as if she's already won the scholarship."

"I don't know what Matt sees in her," Deneen whispered, and grinned. "She's only the prettiest, most popular girl in the school."

Staci shook her head, but she had to smile. A couple years ago, Krystal wouldn't have given Matt so much as a hello. He hadn't been the star—he had barely made the team in the 10th grade. But he had worked hard, and now he was a star as a senior, with girls dying to get to know him.

Rick came back with the refreshments and passed them around. "Sorry, Krystal, they didn't have any diet soda," he said. "I got you a regular cola instead."

"Somebody else will have to drink it," she said, pushing away the paper cup as if it were poison. "I'm on a diet."

"Matt doesn't even like skinny girls," Staci muttered.

Deneen quickly changed the subject. "What are you going to wear to the Galaxy concert, Staci?"

Galaxy was one of the hottest rock groups around, and they were playing in Rancho Grande. Staci and Deneen had stood in line for five hours to get tickets.

"I don't know," Staci said. "I forgot to put my only decent outfit in the wash. I don't know if it'll be clean in time."

"You're hopeless!" Deneen said. "You always put off everything until the very last minute."

She was right, Staci thought. But Deneen drove her crazy, too. Deneen always had to get everything done the day before yesterday. Sometimes, Staci wondered how they stayed friends. Deneen was tiny and red-headed. Staci was tall and brunette. Deneen was super neat. She even cleaned her room without being told. Deneen didn't seem to have any faults, and that, Staci decided, was enough to give anybody a complex.

"Anyway, I might not have to worry about what to wear," Staci added. "Dad says I can't go unless I get at least a *B* on my next English test. I keep getting marked down mostly because of my spelling and grammar."

"Maybe you should get a computer with a program that has spelling and grammar checks," Deneen said.

"Hmm, that's not a bad idea," Staci said.

"If you don't bring up your grades, you'll never get into the Academy," Rick told her.

"You sound like my dad," Staci said. "I wish everybody would get off my case. I'm trying."

"Look, here comes the team!" someone yelled. And the crowd cheered as the players took the field.

The second half was a nightmare for Rancho Grande. Even though Lincoln wasn't a very good team, Matt's team struggled. And Matt had his worst game of the season. He usually scored a couple of touchdowns a game. But he looked sluggish.

"I think that big ape hurt Matt in the first half," Staci said.

Rick nodded. "Maybe. Whatever it is, he's not having a very good game."

When the coach took Matt out in the last quarter, Staci lost interest in the game. Her mind drifted to the story she was writing for her English class. If it was good enough, she had a chance to win the scholarship.

Rancho Grande won by four points. But everybody was a little glum as they made their way out of the crowded stands.

"We should have beaten Lincoln by 30 points," a man in front of them said.

As usual after home games, some of the Rancho Grande students went to a local pizza parlor to hang out "We'll save you seats," Rick said to Staci and Deneen, as he was going to get a ride with another group.

Staci's mother came up with Deneen's and Rick's parents. "Do you girls want a ride home?" she asked.

"We're going to get pizza," Staci said. "Krystal and Matt are taking us."

"All right, but go easy on the cheese," her mother said. "Watch that cholesterol."

"Don't be late," Deneen's dad told them.

As soon as their parents turned away, Staci rolled her eyes at Deneen. "How can you go easy on the cheese? I mean, that's mostly what a pizza is! There wouldn't be anything left! My mom, the health nut."

"Sometimes they treat us like little kids," Deneen answered.

"My brother is eighteen," Staci said. "They won't even let him buy a car." Her dad had insisted that Matt save most of his money for college. The rest Matt spent on his exercise equipment.

Deneen, Krystal and Staci waited for Matt to shower and change. "Want to come with me to the mall tomorrow?" Deneen asked Staci. "*Teen Toggery* is having a sale."

"I don't have the money," Staci answered. "Anyhow, I want to use the computer at school. I have to work on my story."

"Take my advice and don't buy anything from that shop," Krystal told Deneen. "They only sell junk."

Behind Krystal's back, Deneen made a motion as if she were wringing somebody's neck. "My sentiments exactly," whispered Staci .

When Matt finally came out, he looked unhappy. A bunch of young kids ran up to Matt, asking for his autograph. Even a bad game didn't seem to make them think any less of him.

Rick's little brother Bobby said, "Coach should have let you take the ball, instead of kicking it at the end of the half!"

"I wish I had muscles like you," another boy said. "I'll bet you could bend a steel bar."

"Hey, guys, Matt's tired," Krystal said to the boys. She took Matt's arm.

He jerked away from her. "I'm never too tired to sign autographs," he said, snapping at her.

When the boys finally left, Krystal said, "We're all going to the pizza parlor."

"I'm in training," he said. "I just want to get home."

"Oh. Well, I don't blame you," Krystal said, as if she were talking to a small child. "Matt, eating greasy old pizza is not good for you, anyway."

Matt scowled and unconsciously touched the pimples on his neck. Staci knew he was upset by them. Krystal was about as sensitive as Godzilla, she thought.

"My car's close by," Krystal said in a soothing voice. "You'll feel better once you relax and eat something. You don't have to order pizza. You could get a nice, healthy salad like I always do."

He scowled again. "I'm not hungry."

Staci quickly changed the subject. "Uhh, do you feel okay, Matt? Did that big tackler hurt you?"

He swung around and glared at her. "Nobody hurt me!" he said, almost yelling.

Staci backed away, startled by his sudden anger. "But I—I thought that's why the coach took you out."

"I don't want to talk about it," Matt cried. "Why don't you all just leave me alone!" He stalked off, with Krystal running after him.

Staci was hurt and embarrassed. He'd never spoken to her that way before.

"Boy, he's sure in a lousy mood," Deneen said. "He's usually got a smile for everybody."

"He's been tired a lot lately," she said to Deneen, apologizing for him.

But as she watched Matt leave, she wondered what was really bugging him. He sure hadn't been himself.

"Come on," Staci said with a sigh. "We'd better catch up with Rick, or we'll have to walk home."

Two

"HAL, stop your begging," Staci said to the golden Lab staring up at her with his soulful brown eyes while she ate her breakfast. Hal was a stray Matt had brought home a few years ago. Because of the dog's bad breath, Matt had named him Halitosis—Hal for short. "Matt, did you forget to feed him this morning?" Staci asked.

"No—yes—I don't know." Matt stirred his hot cereal, then slammed down his spoon. "Can't we ever have something else besides this slop?"

"Matt Malloy! I won't have you talking like that," his mother said. "Just because you had a bad game last night doesn't give you a license to be rude."

Staci agreed with Matt. Once in a while, she wished they could have bacon and eggs, fried potatoes, and doughnuts. But their mother worked in a health food store, and didn't believe in eating fats and sweets.

"I'm sorry, Mom," Matt said softly. "I'm not hungry."

"I don't think you're getting nearly enough calories," Mrs. Malloy told him.

"It seems to me you've been picking at your food lately," Mr. Malloy said. "Maybe you should see Dr. Abrams."

"I'm fine," Matt said. "I probably forgot to take my vitamins."

"Your grandfather didn't need vitamins," Mr. Malloy said, glancing at his wife. They had a running argument about the value of vitamins and health foods. "He wasn't on a health kick, and he was strong as an ox."

"Yes, and he died at 38 from a heart attack caused by clogged arteries," Mrs. Malloy said. "I don't want that to happen to Matt."

Staci never knew her grandfather, Monroe Malloy, but she felt as if he lived with them. The Great Mongo, as he was called, had played a couple of seasons with the Los Angeles Rams before he hurt his leg and had to retire from football. His pictures and trophies were everywhere throughout the house.

Mr. Malloy continued, "Matt could take a few lessons from—"

"Can't we ever talk about anything besides

the wonderful Mongo Malloy?" Matt asked his father sarcastically.

Staci knew Matt was tired of always being compared with his famous grandfather. She quickly changed the subject.

"Dad," she asked, "do you think we could get a computer? It's a pain to have to borrow my teacher's all the time."

"You'll have to wait, honey," her father said. "We have too many expenses right now."

Every extra penny went into the quick-print shop her dad had just opened. He still worked part-time at the newspaper. So they didn't see much of him.

"Well, if we're so broke, how come Matt can buy new training equipment?" Staci asked. "His room already looks like a gymnasium."

"You know why," her father said with a loud sigh. "If Matt does well this year, he's bound to get a scholarship to a good university. You know he's already received letters expressing interest, but the college coaches want big strong kids."

By a good university, Staci knew he meant academically good, not just a jock mill where the athletes didn't learn anything. Because his dad had died so young, Ed Malloy hadn't been able to go to college. Staci knew he felt terrible because he couldn't afford to send

19

Matt to college.

But Staci wasn't really angry about Matt's gym equipment. Far from it. She was so proud of him that she'd do almost anything to help.

"You'll get your turn," her mother said. "You're only a freshman. You still have plenty of time."

"But I don't, Mom. I have to have my story turned in by the middle of November. About a million other kids use Mr. Knight's computer. I'll never get my story done in time."

"We have a perfectly good typewriter that I used in high school," her father said.

"Da-a-ad!" Staci groaned. "That typewriter belongs in a museum. It doesn't even have a spell checker!"

"We have a spell checker in the bookcase," he said.

"Huh? We do?"

"It's called a dictionary, Staci," he answered. "You might try getting acquainted with it."

"You just don't want me to go to the Academy," Staci said grumbling. "You don't want me to spend the whole summer away from home."

"That's not it at all," her mother said. "We asked you not to try for it this year, but you went right ahead."

Staci had figured that once she won the scholarship, they'd be so proud of her that they wouldn't object.

Her father picked up his dishes, took them to the sink, and rinsed them. "Even if your tuition is paid, it will cost a lot of money. Maybe next year the business will do better and we can afford it."

"I can stay with Aunt Sharon," Staci said. "It won't cost anything but bus fare."

"Look, we don't have time to deal with this now," her mother said. "Your father and I are running late. Will you and Matt please clean up the kitchen? Matt, will you check the shower drain today? I think it's getting clogged. And, Miss Putoffski," she said to Staci, "clean out your closet. You were supposed to do it last week."

Later, as she and Matt were doing the dishes, he said, "Sorry about the computer. When I get rich and famous, I'll buy you anything you want."

Staci thought about how he'd always stood up for her. When she was little and anybody teased her or took her toys, they had to deal with Matt. Most of her friends fought and argued with their brothers and sisters. But she and Matt didn't.

"I haven't told Mom and Dad, but I'd love to

finish high school at the Academy. If I could go to a place like that, I bet I could become a writer. Maybe I could win the Pulitzer Prize."

He gave her long hair a playful yank. "You and your daydreams. But at least you don't tell those crazy stories the way you used to." He laughed. "Remember the time you told the teacher you were late for school because a burglar had broken into the house and tied us all up."

She grinned, remembering some of the wild tales she'd told. "It just proves I should be a writer," she said. "Even that psychologist Mom took me to said it showed I definitely had a great imagination."

As they stood side by side at the sink, she looked up at him. Not too long ago, they'd been almost the same height. Now he was over six feet tall and broad shouldered, weighing 215 pounds. Even his voice was much deeper and gruffer. Just let some kid give me a hard time, she thought, smiling to herself. One look at him and they'd back off fast—really fast.

Right now, though, she noticed that his face looked bloated and slightly greenish. He kept swallowing hard and licking his lips.

"Matt, are you sure you're okay?" she asked. "Maybe Dad's right. Maybe you should go to see the doc—"

He slammed down the dish he was wiping and tore out of the room. Hal raced after him, his toenails clicking on the linoleum. Hearing Matt throw up, she hurried to the bathroom. "Matt, can I do anything?" she called.

"Just leave me alone!"

She slumped to the floor in the hall next to Hal. She put her arm around the dog. "Why do guys have to be so macho?" she asked him. "Why can't they just admit they're sick?"

When Matt finally came out, he held onto the door for a minute. She jumped up ready to help him.

He waved her off. "I'm okay, Stace. I guess I caught the flu. One of those guys from Lincoln must have breathed germs on me at the bottom of a pile up," he said with a weak grin.

She gave a sigh of relief. "I'm glad that's all it is. I was getting kind of worried."

He flexed his biceps. "I'm too tough to get anything worse than a flu bug," he added with a laugh.

"Sure," she said. "Why don't you lie down? I'll finish up in the kitchen."

He flopped on his bed with a groan, pushing aside several muscle magazines. "Wake me up before you go over to school," he said. "I have a team meeting."

"You can't go to a meeting with the flu. I'll call the coach and tell him you can't make it."

"No. I'll take it easy. Coach wants to go over the mistakes we made last night."

"Well," she said doubtfully, "you be careful. I only have one brother, you know."

She closed the door quietly and went back to the kitchen. When she finished her Saturday chores, she hurried to school. On Saturdays from 10 to 3:30, students could use the English teacher's computer for an hour each. Jill, a student from Staci's English class, was using it, staring at the screen. Staci fidgeted until Jill finished.

Jill sighed. "I just can't seem to come up with any ideas."

"That's not exactly my problem," Staci said. "I have so many ideas, I'll have to live to the year 3000 to write them all down."

As soon as Jill left, Staci signed the clipboard and wrote down the time. The computer had a hard drive with directories. She punched up the MALLOY directory, but found no files listed under it. She panicked. Where was the story she'd worked on for two hours on Wednesday?

She couldn't remember having given it a file name. *Maybe I forgot to save it!* she thought. She remembered that she had been

24

late, and her teacher, Mr. Knight, had told her she had to stop for the day. It *had* to be somewhere in the computer's memory.

Mr. Knight had told them never to go into anyone else's files, but this was an emergency. She started going through all the different directories, searching for her story. Most of the file names made no sense, and so she had to go into each one. *It just had to be somewhere!*

After she had looked through at least a dozen, she came to one named XM, and brought it up on the screen.

1. Why do you think the antagonist in...

Oh, no! she thought They were the questions for Monday's English test!

She quickly hit the exit key before she could read too much. Feeling guilty, even though it was an accident, she looked around to see if anyone had come into the room. No one would believe that she wasn't trying to cheat.

She searched quickly through the other directories, her panicky feeling intensifying, and then, she finally found the story in the "Untitled" directory. It had been assigned a number when she had saved it. She sank back in the chair, almost limp with relief.

She'd felt the same way when Hal was lost for two days. She began to read what she'd written on Wednesday.

TERROR IN THE GREAT DIZMAL SWAMP
by Staci Malloy

The girl flead along the pineneedled path. She held her fist over her mouth to mufle the sound ofof her ragged breathing. The moon was her enemy now. If she could see her evil persewer, he could see her.

Ahead of her stretched the forest, dark trunks of black gum and swamp maple. She plunged into the darknes. It it was quiet. Close. Hummid. The only sounds were the stirrings of tiny bats and the whirr of insects. A chill skittered down her spine. Ghosts and vampires and werewolves seemed only to real here in the Great Dizmal Swamp.

Suddenlly her foot sunk into the ooze to the top of her boots. She tried to pull free but the cold mud sucked at her leg.

She knew there were lots of errors, but she decided to correct them later. The three paragraphs had taken her nearly two hours to write. It was going to take a month to write ten pages, and she didn't have that much time. She had the hook, but she wondered how in the world would she get the girl out of the quicksand.

Mr. Knight had always said to write about what you know, she told herself. *I sure don't know anything about swamps or North Carolina, and I don't think there are any swamps in Southern California.* "But I also don't know about anything else," she moaned. "Nothing interesting ever happens to me."

Anyway, Mr. Knight always said a story should say something. TERROR IN THE GREAT DIZMAL SWAMP was just an adventure story. Usually, Staci had a million ideas buzzing around in her head. But today she couldn't come up with anything.

"Maybe I should write a children's story," she said. "I still remember what it was like to be a kid. A Halloween story about a haunted house might be good." She thought for a while, then began to type.

THE DESsERTED OLD HOUSE
by Staci Malloy

Blackbery vines and wild roses hid the desserted old house from the busy street. A broken FOR SALE sign laid amung the tall weads. Under the the cool shade of pine and maple trees, children played taq and hide and seek.

The Old House chukled silently at the children's squeels of laughter. Lonq ago it's family had lived inside. Now it was desserted. Lonly. Except when the children came to play.

Suddenlly a small boy wandered clos to the well in the back yard. Someone had kicked aside the planks. The boy walked closer. And closer.

The Old Houses rafters quivered with feer for him. OOOOOH! it cried out. OOOOOH!

The children looked around. "What was that?"

"Ghosts!" someone shouted.

She wrote several pages, but wasn't happy with that story, either. For some reason, she couldn't concentrate. She stared out the window for a few minutes, watching the wind pick yellow-brown leaves off the trees.

Absent-mindedly, she began to type again. *XMXMXMXMXM*. She looked at the screen. *XM!*

Horrified, she erased the letters. "Darn it! Why did I have to see that file?" It was so tempting to take one little peek at the English test. "Forget it, Malloy," she told herself. "You've never cheated before in your life—

and you're not going to start now!"

She decided to forget about the story until after Monday's exam. This time she saved the file and remembered to give it a name, then exited from the system.

Feeling proud of herself for not looking at the test questions, she signed out. *I wonder if I can catch up with Deneen at the mall?* she asked herself.

As she came out the door, she almost bumped into Krystal. Startled, she gasped. "What are you doing here?"

"Waiting for you," Krystal said. Her voice sounded serious. "I want to talk to you?"

"I'm in kind of a hur—"

"This is important," Krystal said. "It's about Matt."

What did he do? Look at another girl? Staci wanted to ask. Instead, she said, "Okay. What about him?"

"He isn't acting like himself. He's angry all the time. I called him this morning, and he wouldn't talk to me. I, uh, just need to know if it's me, or if something's wrong."

Staci looked at her in surprise. Krystal with a K was actually thinking about someone besides herself.

"I don't think it's anything to worry about," Staci told her. "Matt just has the flu bug."

Krystal gave a relieved smile. "After he had a bad nosebleed the other day, I was afraid he might be sick."

"No, he says he's fine. I sometimes get nosebleeds when we have really dry weather."

"Right. Well, thanks, Staci." Krystal said. "I hope you won't be mad at me when I get the scholarship."

Her good feeling about Krystal disappeared in an instant. "Don't make too many plans," Staci told her. "I have just as good a chance as you do."

Three

"YOU'LL never guess what I discovered," Staci said to Rick and Deneen on their way to school Monday.

"A new way to fix your popcorn?" Rick said. He always teased her about her addiction to popcorn.

"Nope. I accidentally found Mr. Knight's test in the computer."

Deneen stopped. "You didn't *look* at it, did you?"

"Of course not." She grinned. "It was tempting, though. All I saw was part of the first question about one of the stories we've read."

"Did you tell Mr. Knight?" Rick asked.

"Are you kidding? He might think I did look at the questions. He'd never let any of us kids use his computer again."

"I sure hope you get a good grade," said Deneen.

"Don't worry," Staci said confidently. "There's no way I'd miss the Galaxy concert. I used all my baby-sitting money for that ticket."

When they reached school, they went to their separate classes. Staci headed for Mr. Knight's room. He was already there, running something on his printer.

She took her seat in the second row of chairs. Every time she saw him, she wished she were older. He was tall, at least six-foot-four, with black curly hair, brown eyes and a great tan. She thought he was better looking than any of the guys in school. All the girls had a crush on him. Staci knew for a fact that the only reason some of the girls went to the football games was to watch Mr. Knight on the sidelines as the assistant coach.

"As you know," he said as he passed out the test papers, "you may use your dictionaries."

Staci groaned. She'd forgotten to bring hers.

"You have the entire period to finish," he said. "So don't try to rush."

There were only five essay questions. *This is a cinch*, Staci thought as she quickly wrote out her answers. She finished the questions before anyone else, and knew she'd answered them well. *Who needed to cheat, anyhow? Concert, here I come!*

* * * * *

When Mr. Knight gave back the test papers on Friday, Staci sat back in shock. A large red *D* stared at her! The pages were covered with so many red pencil marks that they looked as if they had some terrible disease. She fumed all through her other classes. As soon as school let out, she charged into Mr. Knight's room and slapped the test pages down on his desk.

"Mr. Knight, what's going on? My essay answers were great. Why did I get a D?"

"Take a look at all those misspelled words, Staci. I told everyone they could use a dictionary. You chose not to bring one."

"I forgot," she mumbled. "Anyhow, I thought grammar was only a third of the grade."

"It is. I took off extra points for carelessness." He picked up a page. "Look at the mistakes. You had plenty of time to correct them. Instead, you sat there daydreaming."

"That's not fair," Staci protested. "I'll bet you didn't do that with the other kids."

"I certainly did. But in some ways maybe I am tougher on you because you tell me you want to be a writer. I'd like to see you get a chance at that Academy scholarship, but you'll never make it with this kind of sloppy work."

Staci knew he was right. "I'm sorry, Mr. Knight," she said. "I'll try harder next time."

"If you want to take these home this weekend and correct every mistake, I'll bring your grade up to a *B*."

"But that's too late—" she said.

"Too late for what?"

"For the Galaxy concert. My dad said I can't go if I don't get a good grade."

"You bring the corrected answers back tomorrow by noon, and I'll change the grade."

"Thanks, Mr. Knight. I really appreciate this." She grabbed up the pages. "I promise I'll do better from now on."

After school, she and Rick walked home together. Fridays, Deneen stayed for Jazz Band. "You guys might have to go to the concert without me," Staci said. "I have to correct my English test by noon tomorrow, and if I don't get a better grade, I won't be able to go."

"Hey, I'm really sorry," Rick told her. "Maybe you can get it finished in time."

She shook her head. "No way. It'll take me forever."

"Want me to try to sell your ticket?" he asked. "I know some kids who want to go."

"I guess—wait. You have a grammar and spelling checker on your computer, don't you?"

"Well, yes, but I don't think that's what Knight wants—"

"I still have to do the corrections. It'll just be lots faster."

"It seems like cheating, though."

"We get to use our calculators in math, don't we? It's the same thing. Please, Rick? I have to baby-sit tonight, but I could come over early in the morning."

"Well, okay," he said. "But don't ring the doorbell. My mom sleeps late on Saturdays."

When Staci got home, she checked the kitchen blackboard for messages. She found one from her mother. It said, *Staci—I'm going right from work to help your dad finish a print job. Warm up the spaghetti and fix a salad for yourself and Matt. Love you, Mom.*

She heard Matt in his room and went to see if he wanted to eat early. On game nights, sometimes he didn't eat until afterward. The door was slightly ajar. She knocked, then walked in.

"Matt—"

He swung around and dropped an open bottle of pills on the floor. She hardly recognized her brother's angry, red face.

"Who said you could come into my room?" he yelled at her.

"The—the door was partly open. I wasn't

35

trying to sneak up on you." She started to pick up some of the pills.

"Don't touch those!" he shouted.

Staci backed away.

"I don't know why people can't leave me alone!"

Shocked and hurt, tears filled Staci's eyes. "Matt, I only—"

"Get out!" he screamed, gave her a push and slammed the door.

For a moment, Staci leaned against the closed door. She dried her eyes on her sleeve. Slowly she returned to the kitchen, but she just sat on a stool staring at the counter.

Krystal was right. Something was wrong with Matt. Never in her life had she seen him so angry and out of control. She sat there for a long time trying to decide what to do. She had just made up her mind to call her dad when Matt came into the kitchen.

Avoiding her eyes, he said, so low she could hardly hear him, "I'm sorry I blasted you that way, Stace."

He came over to her and hugged her. She winced. He was so strong, he could easily break her ribs.

"Take it easy," she said with a pained grin. "Save your tackling for the game."

He flexed his muscles. "I just don't know

my own strength."

She looked up at him, now seriously. "Matt, what's wrong? You've never acted like that before."

He rubbed his neck and shoulders. "I guess I got hurt worse in the last game than I thought. I was just taking some aspirin. The pain has been driving me crazy."

"You could have a broken bone or torn a muscle. You should go to the doctor."

He shook his head. "No way. Coach might not let me play."

"Are you nuts? Your health is more important than a game."

He didn't answer for a minute. "Getting a scholarship to a good school is more important than anything to me. *And* to Dad," he said. He gripped her arms until it hurt. "I'll put up with pain, with anything, to get it."

His eyes looked too bright, his face feverish. She pulled away and looked at her arms, expecting to see red marks where Matt had grabbed her.

"And then what?" she asked. "What do you really want to do when you graduate from college? Are you going to be a pro player like Grandpa?"

"No way. Football is just my passport to going to college and getting a degree. I'm not sure what I want to do. Maybe I'll even be a scientist, or an astronomer."

Staci thought about how, before he got into football, all Matt was interested in was astronomy and his telescope. He'd even painted the solar system on his bedroom ceiling.

"Good," she said. "I'm glad you're not going to stay in football. I can hardly stand to watch whenever you get tackled. Krystal is worried about you, too."

He glared at her. "How come you two are discussing me?" he asked.

"We both think you're pushing yourself too hard," Staci explained. "You spend hours at practice, then more hours working out either at the gym or in your room. I hardly ever see you with your old friends."

"Aw, they're jerks," he said, dismissing them with a wave of his hand. "I don't have time to fool around with a bunch of losers."

His face started to turn red again, and Staci changed the subject. "When do you want to eat? We're having spaghetti."

"I don't want anything," he said. "I'm going to rest until I have to leave for the game."

"Good idea. Let the aspirin work."

"What? Oh, yeah. Right." He started to leave, then turned back to her. "Staci, do me a favor, and don't say anything to Mom about

38

the aspirin, okay? You know how she is about taking anything except vitamins."

Staci nodded. "I won't say anything. Matt, I'm sorry Mom and I won't be at the game tonight. She's working with Dad, and I have to baby-sit."

"Won't be much of a game, anyhow," he said. "We're going to beat Union by twenty points."

"Take care tonight," Staci added. "I don't want you to get hurt. Try to stay out of the way of those big steroid geeks."

He gave her a long look. Then he laughed. "Where did you hear that expression?"

"It must have been at the last game. Deneen thought that big guy that hurt you was cute. Rick called him a steroid geek."

"Yeah, I guess maybe there are some kids who use steroids. Well, I'm going to lie down." Then he grinned and added, "I think I'd better get a DO NOT DISTURB sign for my door."

"Don't worry. I won't barge in again."

When he left the room, she felt a little better. *But why should he get so angry all the time?* she thought. No matter how much he protested, she was sure something was wrong.

Four

"SORRY I'm late," Staci whispered as Rick let her in the door the next morning.

"No need to be quiet now," Rick said. "Everybody's been up for hours."

"I'm sorry I'm late," Staci explained. "Matt was telling me about last night's game, and I sort of lost track of the time."

"I thought you wanted to correct your essay test," he said gruffly. "Come on into the study."

"Are you mad at me?" she asked, following him.

"No, I'm not mad. I just wish you'd quit goofing around."

He was about the fifth person who'd been irritated with her lately.

"Okay, okay," she said. "I'll be so perfect from now on, you won't know me."

Rick grinned. "Don't get carried away. You

don't have to be like Deneen."

The study was lined with bookshelves. Staci had seen *libraries* with fewer books. Rick was always studying some new subject. Just as they were getting settled, Bobby poked his head in the room. "Hey, Staci, do you think Matt would autograph my new football?" he asked.

"Sure he will," she replied, "but I wouldn't bother him today."

Matt was Bobby's hero, and she didn't want him to catch Matt at a bad time. "If you want, I'll take it and get him to sign it."

Bobby reluctantly held out the football to her. "Okay, but tell him to put 'To Bobby Wagner, the next Matt Malloy.'"

"Now beat it, Pee Wee," Rick said. "Staci has work to do."

He turned on the computer for her. Luckily, he used the same word processing software that Mr. Knight used. So, she was familiar with the program. While she started typing her test answers into the computer, Rick sat on the floor, looking through a science magazine. Except for his long legs, Staci thought he looked like his kid brother reading a comic book.

"Rick, aren't you afraid you'll fill your head with so much information, there won't be any room left by the time you're twenty-one?" she asked.

"Well, I like to know about a lot of things."

She shook her head. "I think you should be an encyclopedia salesman."

"Nope," he said. "I'm going to be a detective and solve the mystery of why Staci Malloy can't keep her mind on her work."

"Better make that a brain surgeon—or even a psychiatrist."

Rick gave Staci a stern look, and she said quickly, "I'm working, I'm working."

Staci concentrated on typing in her essay answers, then used the spell checker. It caught a dozen misspelled words, even a couple Mr. Knight hadn't marked. Next, she used the grammar checker. The checker highlighted the very first line and said the sentence was too long. That was easy to fix. It marked the second line, saying she had split an infinitive. She fixed that. The checker said she used too many passive sentences, ended too many with a preposition, used vague adverbs, wrong capitalization, redundant words, trite phrases, and was long-winded.

"Rick, I hate this grammar checker!" she cried. "It tells me I'm doing all these things wrong, but it doesn't tell me how to fix them."

"You're supposed to figure that out yourself." He got up and took a book off the shelf. "Here's a college English handbook. It should explain what you need to do."

"But that's going to take hours," she moaned. "I won't get it done by noon."

"You should have thought of that this morning instead of talking about football."

"Rick, you're good in English. How about helping me?"

He shook his head. "Sorry. I have to meet Jeremy in a few minutes."

"Can't you call him and say you'll be a little late?"

"Not this time, Staci. Deneen and I made a pact last night. Neither of us is going to help you get out of predicaments that you get yourself into."

"You just ended a sentence with a preposition," she said, teasing him.

"I'm serious, Staci. You're on your own. This is a test. It's supposed to show what *you* know. Be sure to turn off the computer and printer when you're through." And without a backward glance, he left the study.

"Some friend you are!" she yelled.

She worked on the test until 11:45, making as many corrections as she could, then printed it out. She grabbed up the pages, thanked Rick's mom, rushed out of the house and raced to school.

Mr. Knight's door was locked when she got to school. She peered through the window at the clock. 12:16.

* * * * *

The phone was ringing when Staci came in the kitchen door. She hurried to answer.

"Hi, it's me," Deneen said. "Have you figured out what you're going to wear tonight?"

"Yeah. My pajamas," Staci said. "I can't go."

"Oh no! Because of your English grade?"

"What else?"

"I'm really sorry, Staci. Can't you get your dad to change his mind?"

"He wouldn't change his mind. Anyway, I didn't want to go all that much." She didn't want Deneen to feel sorry for her. "I was only going because I know how much you're into music."

"Well, I'll come by tomorrow and tell you all about it," Deneen said. "Do you want to sell the ticket?"

"Sure, somebody might as well get some good out of it. I may not be home. So I'll leave it in the mailbox, and you can pick it up on the way. Well, I have to go. I have a million things to do today."

After she hung up, she wandered around the house, feeling sorry for herself. The phone rang. *Maybe it was Rick,* she thought, *calling to apologize for not helping her.* It was only Krystal.

"Staci, is Matt there?"

"No, I haven't seen him since breakfast."

"Oh..."

Staci remembered their conversation about Matt. "Is something wrong?" she asked.

"We had a big argument last night. He got mad over nothing. He just isn't like himself lately."

"He's under a lot of stress during football season," Staci told her, "especially since he's so worried about getting a scholarship. I think you're getting excited over nothing."

"Well, maybe. Would you have him call me when he gets home?"

"Sure," Staci answered. But after she hung up, she realized she wasn't sorry that Matt and Krystal had had a fight.

Staci checked the message board to see if there was a message about Matt. It said her mom and dad wouldn't be home until late. *So what was new?* she thought. These days, they were hardly ever home for dinner. Nothing about Matt.

She went to the back door and whistled for Hal. "Come on in, boy. You don't talk much, but you're better company than some people I know."

The dog charged into the house, barking happily. With the dog in her lap, she watched an old movie on TV. "Maybe I should be a screenwriter," she said to Hal. "The movies probably don't worry about your spelling and grammar."

Hal just stared at her.

"Better yet, maybe I should be an actress. Writing stories is just like acting. You have to become all the characters."

Hal growled.

"Okay. Bad idea," Staci said.

"What's a bad idea?"

Staci jumped at the sound of Matt's voice. "I didn't hear you come in. You scared me."

He switched on a light. "What are you doing here in the dark? Why aren't you getting ready for the concert?"

She explained why she couldn't go. "But it's no big deal," she said.

"Right. You've only been looking forward to this concert for months. Hey, I have a great idea. Let's get us some hamburgers, fries, and milk shakes. I'll stop by the video store and find a good horror movie. We'll make

46

popcorn and—"

"Cut it out," she said, thinking he was teasing. "Like you're going to break training *and* your date with Krystal." She hit her forehead with her palm. "Oops, I forgot. Krystal wants you to call her."

"It won't kill me to eat some junk food," Matt said. "As for Krystal, I'll talk to her later."

"Maybe you should call her now," Staci said. "She sounded pretty upset."

He went into the kitchen, with the dog loping along behind. Hal was probably hoping to get something to eat—as usual. Since the house was small, Staci couldn't help hearing Matt's side of the conversation.

"It's me," he said in a flat tone of voice. "Staci said you called." There was a long pause, then he said coldly, "There's nothing to talk about...No. I have plans for tonight...Yes, it's another girl—Staci!...Krystal, just get off my back!...No!...Goodbye."

When Staci heard him slam down the phone, she walked to the kitchen door.

"I wish people would just leave me alone!" Matt said, almost growling.

She nodded. "I know what you mean. Rick and Deneen have been giving me a bad time."

He came over and put his arm around her

shoulder. "As long as there's the two of us, we don't need anybody else."

"Right," she agreed. "It's us against the world."

Hal gave a long pitiful whine, and they both laughed. "You too, pal," Matt said, mussing the dog's hair. "The three Malloys." Hal ran around in circles, barking happily.

"I'm going after the video and our dinner," Matt said. "Do you want some onions on your hamburger?"

"Sure," Staci said. "And I'll make a ton of popcorn."

This is going to be about the best night ever, she thought as Matt drove off to get the food and movie. *Krystal was wrong about Matt. He hasn't changed at all. He is just like always, the best brother—and the best friend— a girl could have!*

Five

STACI was taking a turkey meat loaf out of the oven one evening the next week, when Rick knocked on the back door. She was surprised to see him. They hadn't talked much since the Galaxy concert. "Come on in," she said.

He seemed nervous.

"What's up?" she asked.

"Uhh, can I borrow your mom's Bundt pan. Mom wants to bake a cake tomorrow for a church dinner."

As Staci dug the pan out of a cupboard, Rick sniffed. "That smells good," he said, nodding at the meat loaf. "I didn't know you could cook."

"I'm learning. Mom and Dad don't get home until after nine most nights." She handed him the Bundt pan.

"I guess the new print shop takes a lot of

49

work," he said. Staci knew he was just trying to make conversation.

"That's for sure." She took the baked potatoes out of the oven, and turned it off.

"Well, I guess I should get home and shove something in the microwave," he said as he eyed the potatoes. "Mom and Dad went to dinner and a movie. Since Bobby's sleeping over at a friend's house, I told them that I could take care of myself tonight."

Even though Rick could probably feed himself, Staci thought he wanted some company. "We have plenty, Rick. Want to stay and eat with Matt and me?"

"That'd be great," Rick answered quickly. "If you're sure you have enough."

"I made enough to feed the whole football team." She got another plate from the cupboard. "Matt," she called. "Dinner's ready."

"Staci, about the other day..." Rick avoided her eyes. "You know, I didn't intend for you to miss the concert when I didn't help you with your test."

"That's okay. I understand. Deneen gave me a blow-by-blow description of the concert. Anyhow, Matt and I had a great time."

"Then you're not mad at me?" he asked.

She shrugged. "No, I'm not. Don't worry about it. Anyway, I finished the corrections and turned my paper in last Monday. He raised my grade to a *B*."

"I'm glad. Hey, anytime you want to use my computer to write your story, just holler. Okay?"

"Thanks. I will. Matt!" she called again, louder this time. "Dinner's getting cold."

"Can I use your bathroom to wash up?" Rick asked.

"Sure. You know where it is," Staci said. "I guess I'd better get Matt. When he's lifting weights, he doesn't hear anything."

Rick went into the bathroom opposite Matt's room. Staci knocked on Matt's door and said, "Matt? Didn't you hear me call?"

"Go away!" Matt's voice sounded muffled.

"What do you mean, go away? Matt Malloy, I slaved over a hot—"

Matt rushed out of his room and headed for the bathroom. A bloody T-shirt covered his face.

"Matt! Did you cut your—"

He turned the bathroom doorknob just as Rick came out. "Out of my way, Wagner!" Matt yelled through the shirt.

"I'm going to call 9-1-1," Staci said in a shaking voice. There was so much blood!

"No! Mind your own business, Staci. It's just a nosebleed," Matt said as he slammed the door shut.

Staci looked at Rick's face. "Do you think it's really just a nosebleed?" she asked.

Rick looked in Matt's room at the weights Matt had been using. "Probably. I've seen some other kids get them when they're working out."

Staci knocked on the bathroom door. "Matt, are you okay? Can I do anything?"

"Yeah, you can get away from the door and leave me alone," he said, sounding weak.

After a few minutes, he came out of the bathroom. He held a wet towel over his face. When he saw Rick looking at him, Matt growled, "What're you staring at?"

"Maybe you should see a doctor," Rick said. "You might have high blood pressure."

Matt sneered and yelled, "Thank you, Dr. Wagner!" He went into his room and slammed the door so hard that the house shook.

"I'm sorry, Rick," Staci said in a small voice. "Matt hates to have anybody see him when he's sick or hurting."

They headed slowly back to the kitchen. "Maybe I'd better be going," Rick said.

"No, stay. Please."

Rick gave her a long look. "You're not scared of him, are you?"

She gave a harsh laugh. "Are you kidding?

My brother's my best friend. I just don't want to eat alone."

They heard Matt vomiting. "But I just wish he'd see a doctor," she said. "I'm really worried about him."

Neither of them said anything as they dished up their food. She'd forgotten to put the potatoes in the oven before the meat loaf, and they were still hard in the middle. Staci's appetite was gone, anyhow.

Suddenly, Staci pushed her plate away, too upset to eat any more. "Rick, do you really think he could have high blood pressure?"

"A nosebleed is a way for the body to release some of the pressure," Rick said. "If he does have it, he should go to a doctor. It's nothing to fool around with."

"But Matt's so healthy. Mom has taught him all about eating right and taking care of himself."

"Staci, I think..." He paused, then continued. "I hate to say this, but you and your parents ought to be on the lookout for signs of..."

"Rick, what are you talking about?" Staci didn't like the sound of his voice or his serious face. "Signs of what?"

"Anabolic steroids," he said.

"Huh? You mean like that hulk from Lincoln? The one you called a steroid geek?"

Rick nodded.

Staci laughed. "Stop kidding around." She carried her dish over to the sink. "I thought you were serious for a second."

"I'm serious, Staci."

"You're crazy!" she said spinning around angrily. "You know Matt. He's always been against using drugs."

"A lot of kids don't think steroids are drugs. But they *are*. And they're dangerous."

"How do you know so much about them?" she asked sarcastically.

"Because I've read about them. And I know several guys on the football team who use them."

"And has it hurt them?" Staci said angrily. But her anger at Rick was turning into worry for Matt. *Could Rick be right?*

"Steroids affect everybody differently," he said. "They can make you aggressive, even violent. Sometimes it might take years for liver cancer or heart problems to show up."

"Okay, okay, you may be right about steroids. But you're dead wrong about Matt. I *know* he wouldn't use drugs. Just because he has a couple of nosebleeds and loses his temper once in a while, you think my brother's on drugs."

54

"Staci, you can't deny that Matt's changed since this summer."

Krystal's words popped into Staci's head. *He isn't acting like himself,* she had said.

Well, neither Krystal nor Rick knew Matt the way she did, Staci decided. "You know what I think," she said, getting angry at Rick again. "I think you like to spout all this stuff just to show off how much you know."

Rick looked at her for a moment, then shrugged. "So be an ostrich. You're just like Coach Phillips and everybody else. You won't open your eyes and see what's going on." He got up from the table and walked over to the sink, next to Staci, who had been rinsing dishes. "I'll help with the dishes."

"No thanks. I think you'd better go now."

He slipped his jacket on and headed for the door. "Thanks for dinner. And, Staci, at least think about what I said."

She just kept shaking her head. "I don't have to think about it. I know my brother."

After Rick left, Staci hurried to Matt's room. Hal was lying in front of the door. "What's the matter, pooch?" she asked. "Won't Matt let you in?"

She listened at Matt's door, but all she could hear was Matt's loud breathing. He was asleep. Relieved, she whispered, "Good night, Matt."

The next morning after their parents left for work, Matt came into the kitchen. He grabbed a paper bag from under the sink and shoved his bloody shirt and towels into it.

"I don't know when I'll be back," he said, walking out without looking at Staci.

* * * * *

Although Staci tried to put Rick's words out of her head over the next few weeks, she couldn't. She found herself watching Matt whenever he wasn't looking. Except for the added height and weight since last summer, and the acne, he looked like the same old Matt. He was back to eating big meals again, and that made her parents happy. No, she decided, Rick was definitely wrong. Matt couldn't be using steroids.

Besides, she had plenty of other things to worry about. Her grades had dropped, not only in English, but her other classes, too. One Saturday when she was using Mr. Knight's computer to work on her story, he came into the room. "Staci, sorry to interrupt you, but I want to talk to you for a minute."

"Sure, I was having trouble with my story, anyhow."

"Are you still serious about applying for a scholarship to the Academy?" he asked.

"Well, yeah. That's why I want this story to be perfect."

"I'm afraid it will take more than that," he said.

She frowned at the ominous words. "What do you mean?"

"I did some checking, and I see you haven't been doing too well in your classes. Staci, is something bothering you?"

She was tempted to ask Mr. Knight about steroids, but he might guess she was worried about Matt. "No, nothing's bothering me. I, umm, haven't been sleeping very well lately. I have a lot more to do at home because Mom and Dad are working so hard at the print shop. I guess that's why my grades aren't so hot."

He nodded and said, "Well, I just wanted to warn you that the test next week will determine whether you can apply to the Academy. I want you to do well, Staci. I'd be very proud if one of my creative writing students won a scholarship."

"I'll really try, Mr. Knight. I won't let you down."

"I hope not, Staci. I think you'd better do some heavy studying. This test is a rough one."

She gave him a sheepish smile. "Don't worry, Mr. Knight. I promise I won't make a lot of careless mistakes this time."

He gave her a pat on the back. "Good. I have to leave early today for a football team meeting. You can stay an extra hour if you'll turn everything off and lock up for me."

"Oh, sure. That'll be great."

As soon as he left, she went back to her story. But she couldn't keep her mind off what Mr. Knight had said. *This test is a rough one...This test is a rough one...This test...*

She exited from her story, making sure she had saved it. She sat there a long time, just staring at the screen. She hadn't even read the last few assignments. What if she got another *D* on the test? She'd lose her chance at a scholarship for sure. Even worse, she'd be letting Mr. Knight down. He was counting on her. He had even told her how proud he'd be if she won.

Staci groaned. *There isn't time to read everything for the test Monday*, she thought. *If I only knew what a few of the questions were about, it would cut down on the amount of reading. I could concentrate on reading the stuff I knew was going to be on the test.*

She hesitantly changed to Mr. Knight's files. *Maybe there isn't a new XM file,* she thought. *Maybe it's still the one for the last test.* She put the cursor on the XM file. *I'll just take a quick look and see if it's the new test,* she told herself. She brought the file up and saw that it was a different test.

Quickly, she exited from it. Her heart was pounding. She wiped her damp hands on her jeans. She worried about the consequences of cheating. *But if I just looked at the first couple of questions, would that really be cheating? I'd still have to read the books and write the essay answers. It would just give me a little edge, that's all. Is there anything so wrong with that?* She told herself she would just look at a few questions. Then she'd go right home and start reading.

Quickly, before she could change her mind, she brought up the XM file on the screen. She read the first three questions and jotted them down on a piece of paper. She was reading the fourth when she heard the doorknob turning.

She froze. Her heart raced. The door squeaked opened, and she heard footsteps. She spun around to see who was coming in.

Six

"OH," Staci said with relief. She held her hand over her heart. "It's you two."

"So, who were you expecting?" Deneen asked. "An axe murderer?"

"You looked scared to death," Rick said.

Staci tried to laugh, but it sounded hollow, even to her ears. "Uhh, I was just working on my story about a haunted house."

Rick started toward the desk, and Staci quickly exited from the XM file. "What are you guys doing here?" she asked, trying to keep her voice from shaking.

"We came to see if you wanted to go ice skating at the mall," Deneen said.

"I'd love to, but I was just leaving. I have to do a lot of reading." She avoided their eyes. "I have a big exam Monday." She bit her lip, wishing she hadn't mentioned the test.

"Well, you could always look at the test

questions on the computer," Deneen said.

"What do you mean by that?!" Staci said sharply.

"I was just kidding," Deneen said with a strange look on her face. "Boy, are you ever touchy."

Staci turned off the computer and stood up. "I don't think that was very funny. I don't want anybody to think I'm a cheater."

"How come you're so defensive?" Rick asked quietly.

"I don't know what you're talking about." She covered the computer and checked out on the clipboard. "Look, I have to lock up for Mr. Knight. So let's get out of here. Okay?"

"You sure are in a big hurry," Rick said, picking up a piece of paper that fell on the floor. He glanced at the paper, then said, "Here, you forgot this."

Staci's heart sank. It was the paper with the questions written on it. She knew Rick had realized what it was. "Okay, so I did look at the first few questions."

"Staci!" Deneen cried, her face shocked. "You didn't!"

"I wasn't going to look at all of them," Staci answered. "Just enough to give me an edge, a fighting chance to get that scholarship to the Academy."

"I had to work hard to get to the Academy last summer," Deneen said. Her face was red with anger. "I never thought you'd cheat to get there!"

Staci tried to explain about how much Mr. Knight was counting on her. "I don't know why you're making such a big deal out of it. I *still* have to do all the work, write essay answers to all the questions. I just wanted to save myself a little time."

But neither Rick nor Deneen said anything. They just kept staring at her. "Are you going to tell on me?" Staci asked.

After a while, Deneen said, "No."

Rick looked at her for a long time, then whispered, "I thought you were better than that. Like brother, like sister, I guess."

"What do you mean by that?!" Staci said, snapping at him.

"Figure it out for yourself," he said. He spun on his heel and walked out of the room. Without a word, Deneen followed him.

* * * * *

Staci went straight home so that she could start reading the assignments she had put off for so long. She concentrated on the stories Mr. Knight had used for the first four questions on the test. But she kept thinking about what Rick had said.

Like brother, like sister. Was he talking about Matt using steroids? She realized with a start that cheating on a test was pretty much the same as an athlete using illegal drugs. *Just enough to give me an edge,* she had told Rick and Deneen. Could Matt be doing steroids for the same reason?

She wished with all her heart that she hadn't looked at the test questions. She had never thought of herself as a cheater or a bad person. But yet, she failed to resist the temptation. Maybe even a good guy like Matt could be tempted to do something wrong, too—if he thought he needed to do it to get something he really wanted.

She shoved her books aside, telling herself she'd get up at dawn and study. But right now, she had something important to do before the library closed. She rode her bike to the library. There she found three books and a magazine on the subject of steroids, and she hurried home to read them. Nobody was home, but she locked her door anyway. She didn't want anyone—especially Matt—to know she was reading up on steroids.

Anabolic steroids are synthetic variants of

male hormones that help athletes build up muscles faster...Athletes who use steroids can get bigger, stronger and faster than those who don't use them...There is a $100 million-a-year black market in the illegal drug.

As she read, she began to get a sick lump in her stomach. Matt did seem to have some of the minor side effects—nausea, loss of appetite, vomiting, acne and nosebleeds. But using steroids could be more dangerous than even Rick had said. In young people, it could stunt the growth of their height. Steroids could cause sterility so that the user could never have kids. They could also cause liver problems, cancer, heart attacks, high blood pressure, and a tendency toward violence.

One book even said that a death certificate usually wouldn't list steroid use as the cause of death. But it was often the contributing factor.

Staci closed her eyes. *Matt, please don't you be using them. I couldn't take it if something happened to you.*

She was still reading when she heard someone come in the back door. "Anybody home?" her mother called.

Staci shoved the books under her mattress. She unlocked her door and answered, "Just me." She hurried out to the kitchen, where her mother was unloading groceries.

"Give me a hand, honey," her mother said.

"Mom," Staci said, as she put frozen food in the freezer, "I want to ask you something."

"Ask away."

"Mom, do you think Matt seems—"

"There must be another bag in the car," her mother said. "Wait a second."

When her mother returned with the bag, she said, "Now, what about Matt? I can't believe how much he's getting to look like his grandfather. It's almost uncanny."

"Mo-om!"

"I'm sorry, honey. I have so many things on my mind, I feel as if my head is going to explode. Let me make a cup of tea, and then we'll sit and talk."

While her mother boiled water for her herbal tea, Staci poured a glass of milk and opened a package of whole wheat fig bars from the health food store.

Her mother kicked off her shoes and held the hot cup to her face to take a sip. She yawned. "Thank goodness your father and I don't have to work late tonight. I don't know when I've been so tired."

"Maybe it's catching," Staci said. "Have you noticed how tired Matt is lately?"

"I know. I've told him not to overdo it, but he's an overachiever like me." Staci thought her mother sounded proud to be an over-achiever. "When I used to train for a race, I'd always push myself to the limit."

Staci wanted to talk about Matt, not her mother's racing days. "Have you noticed anything different about Matt?" she asked.

"Not really." Her mother leaned back in the chair and closed her eyes. "Different how?"

"I don't know," answered Staci. "He's cranky. He flies off the handle at the slightest thing and doesn't eat like he used to."

"That's not surprising. He's under a lot of pressure during football season, even more so this year with the college scholarship hanging over his head."

"Did you put him on some new vitamins?" Staci asked.

"Nothing new." Her mother opened her eyes and sat up. "Why all these questions? Do you know something I don't?"

"No," Staci said quickly. "Uhh, Matt complained awhile back about hurting."

"Well, football *is* a bruising sport. Your dad said that even the Great Mongo could hardly move the day after a game."

"I just—well, I just wondered if he ought to go to the doctor."

"Oh, he did go. The team physician gave him a complete checkup. Matt said he got a clean bill of health." She smiled. "Matt said the doctor told him that he wished all the kids on the team were as healthy as Matt is."

A great wave of relief swept over Staci. *A doctor would have discovered signs of the steroids if Matt were using them,* she thought. Suddenly, she got angry at Rick for accusing Matt of such a thing. She was even angrier at herself for doubting her brother.

She looked up. Her mother's head had dropped down. She was sound asleep. Feeling happier than she had in several weeks, Staci began to fix dinner.

* * * * *

The more she continued to think about it, however, the angrier Staci got at Rick. *How could he think that Matt was on steroids?* Then she had an even worse thought. *What if he said anything to anyone else?* After dinner, she grabbed her jacket.

"Where are you going?" her mother wanted to know.

"I have something I have to do."

"This is the first evening in months that your dad and I have been home, and you decide to take off. I thought we could watch a movie and maybe make caramel corn."

"That sounds great, Mom," Staci answered. "I'll only be a few minutes. I just have to talk to Rick."

"It sounds important." Her mother gave her a long look. "Is something wrong?"

"No, I just forgot to tell him something."

"But it's so foggy out tonight," her mother said. "Can't you tell him on the phone?"

"No. I definitely have to tell him to his face."

"Okay, but hurry back." Her mother gave her a little smile, and Staci knew she thought it was some boy-girl problem.

All the way to Rick's house on the next block, Staci rehearsed what she wanted to say to him. By the time she got there, she was fuming.

He answered the door when she rang the doorbell. "Hey, what are you doing out in this fog?" he asked.

"I want to talk to you—" She saw his parents in the family room. "In private."

"Sure," he said. "Let's go the study."

She waved to the Wagners and followed Rick to the study.

"Let me take your jacket," he said.

She brushed back her hair, which was damp

from the fog. "No thanks, I won't be here that long," she said.

She took a deep breath and began. "Rick Wagner, you can put me down for cheating on my test. I was wrong, and I'm sorry about it. But you'd better not go around accusing my brother of doing something illegal."

"I haven't 'gone around' accusing him of anything," Rick said. "I just told you that I thought he had all the signs of someone using steroids."

"Well, you were wrong!"

"Well, if that's true, I'm glad about it. But how do you know? Did you ask Matt?"

"No, I didn't need to," said Staci. "The team doctor gave him a complete checkup."

"Team doctor?" Rick said with a frown.

"Yes. If Matt had been using anything, the doctor would have known. So that settles it!"

Rick sighed. "Staci, there's a trainer who takes care of sprains and stuff like that. But there isn't any team doctor."

A chill went down Staci's back. "What? You—you're sure?"

"I'm sure," Rick said. "I'm really sorry, Staci. If Matt told you that, he was lying."

Staci felt her insides go hollow. Then she fled from the house.

Seven

THE next day, Sunday, Staci had planned to study all day. But her mind kept jumping back to Matt. That afternoon, when her parents were out for a few minutes, she stood by Matt's door for a long time, trying to get up the nerve to knock. She felt she *had* to find out the truth. Finally, she tapped and called, "It's me. Can I come in?"

At first he didn't answer. As she started to walk away, he opened the door. He scowled at her as if she were a stranger. "I'm busy," he said.

"I—I just—I need to talk—"

"Not now!" he said and slammed the door.

Tears sprang to her eyes. She hardly recognized Matt sometimes. Returning to her room, she got out the library books. One book said that anabolic steroids were first used during World War II. They were given to German troops to increase muscle strength and aggressiveness. That could certainly explain why usually-happy Matt was angry all the time, she thought.

She read the books on steroids until dinner. After dinner, she put the books aside and studied for the creative writing test. Even though she was sleepy and her eyes were burning, she continued to read until nearly two in the morning. Too tired to even get undressed, she flopped on the bed in her clothes. Once, toward dawn, she awakened from a nightmare about Matt. She couldn't remember the dream—only that it was frightening.

Without eating breakfast, she went out the back door and took a different route to school so that she wouldn't have to face Rick or Deneen. When she sank into her desk at school, she felt confident that she'd do well on the test.

As she answered the first four questions, a pang of guilt stabbed her. *Well, I can't do anything about it now,* she told herself. *It would be stupid not to answer them correctly. Anyway, everybody says I'm going to be a great writer someday. Why should one silly test keep me from getting my dream?* She wrote fast, but carefully corrected her spelling and grammar—even though it was a big pain. When she turned in her paper, Mr. Knight glanced at it. Then he asked her to come to his room after school.

Her stomach tied up in a knot, and she felt sick. *Did he find out that I read some of the test questions?* she wondered. *No, how could he find out?*

The rest of the day dragged on. She nearly fell asleep in algebra class. By the end of the day, she was exhausted and worried, and she wished that she had never looked at those stupid test questions. Staci walked slowly to Mr. Knight's room. He was seated at the desk. She noticed that he was looking at her paper, and her heart dropped to her stomach.

"What did you want to see me about?" she asked, trying to keep her voice steady. "I tried not to make any careless mistakes this time."

He smiled. "You did very well, Staci. I'm proud of you. I haven't quite finished grading your paper, but I'm impressed."

Her stomach returned almost to normal. "Oh, wow, am I glad. I was afraid you were going to bawl me out again."

He shook his head. "I wanted to talk about your brother," he said, laying down her test paper.

"M-Matt? What about him?"

"Do you know if something's going on with

72

him? I've tried to get hold of your folks, but they have not been home. And Matt has a wall around him lately."

Staci had to think fast. She was tempted to tell Mr. Knight what she suspected. But if she did, then Matt might get kicked off the team. Then, goodbye scholarship. She decided that she couldn't tell the assistant coach about his star player. "Well—uh—I think he just has a lot of pressure on him right now," she answered. "He can't afford to go to college unless he gets a scholarship."

Mr. Knight nodded slowly. "I suppose that's part of it. I'm a little worried about his physical condition, though. I tried to get him to see a doctor. He said your family physician had given him a clean bill of health."

Oh, Matt! she thought. *You're lying to everybody now!*

"I know how close you two are," Mr. Knight said. "Maybe you can get him to talk about what's bothering him. If there's any way I can help, let me know."

"Thanks, I will."

He smiled and stood up. "Keep up the good work, Staci."

* * * * *

That evening, before their parents came home, Staci worked up enough courage to confront her brother. The minute he walked through the door after practice, she stopped him.

"Matt, I want to talk to you."

"Later. I'm beat." He tried to push past her, but she grabbed his arm.

A flash of anger passed over his face, so intense that she suddenly was frightened. But she held her ground. "I don't care if you get mad at me. I'm not letting up until we talk."

He sighed, looking tired. "Okay. Come on. Let's get it over with."

She followed him to his room. He flopped on the bed, and she stood looking down at him.

"So, what's up?" he asked.

For a moment, she was silent.

"Look, Stace, you said that you wanted to talk. So talk."

"I want to know why you lied to Mom and to Mr. Knight," she said. "You told Mom you saw the team doctor. I know there isn't one."

"Okay, I lied. She kept harping about seeing a doctor. So, I told a little white lie."

"Is that why you lied to Mr. Knight about seeing Dr. Abrams?"

Matt reared up and swung his feet to the

floor with a bang. "What's the third degree all about?" His face turned red. "How come Coach Knight's talking to you about me?"

"He thinks there's something bothering you, Matt. I'm worried about you. You're mad all the time."

"Sure I'm mad," Matt answered. "I'm sick of everybody always being on my back about something all the time."

"I think it's more than that," she said softly. "You haven't been eating...the nosebleeds and vomiting...the acne."

Suddenly he was still, almost as if he had stopped breathing. "What are you getting at?" he said softly.

"Matt, are you on steroids?"

"Are you crazy?!" he yelled. "Did Knight accuse me of using?"

She shook her head. "No, no way."

"Well, he'd better not accuse me!" Matt said, sputtering.

Staci went over to Matt's dresser and picked up the bottle labeled aspirin.

"What do you think you're doing?" he asked, demanding to know.

"I have a terrible headache." She rubbed her head. "Can I have a couple of your aspirins?" Before he could answer, she unscrewed the lid and took out two small white tablets.

"Put those down!" he said.

"I'll just get a glass of water from the—"

"Give me those!" he said and grabbed the tablets from her hand.

"Why, Matt?" she asked. "Because they aren't aspirin, are they?"

"Okay! Okay! So what if they are steroids? It's just for a little while, just until the football season's over. All I need is a little edge."

Staci froze. Those were the same words she'd used herself about cheating on the English test!

"Matt, I got some books from the library that tell all about what steroids can do to you in just a few weeks or months."

"Aw, those dumb books just try to scare people," answered Matt. "If steroids are so dangerous, how come half the athletes use them? How come they're so easy to get?"

"Where *do* you get them?"

"I can get them in one of the gyms in San Diego. People who work out there get them from Mexico, I guess."

"But don't they cost a lot? Where do you get the money?"

"I've got some money saved up," Matt answered.

"Matt, that money's for college!"

He gave her a wry smile. "If I get a scholarship, I won't need the college money, will I?"

"I just can't believe you'd take drugs," she said. "You've always been against stuff that can hurt your body."

"Staci, they're not *really* drugs. They're just hormones that help build muscle. Anyway, if there are some side effects, they won't happen to me. You know how healthy I am."

"Matt, you're kidding yourself!" she cried. "Why can't you understand? You probably already have high blood pressure. What about those nosebleeds you had?"

"I felt okay the next day. And I went down to the drugstore and got one of those blood pressure checks. Mine was fine."

"What if it goes up? What if you have an even worse nosebleed? What if you—"

"Staci, I told you. I'll only take them until the season's over."

"Please, Matt," she pleaded. "Stop now."

"I can't. I tried, but I started losing my strength. I lost weight. I have to keep using them until I get that scholarship."

"But why? Why do you have to do something that might hurt you?"

"You want to know why?" Matt asked with fire in his eyes. "You want to know why I have to be the best? I'll tell you why. Because Dad's counting on me. Coach Phillips is counting on me. This whole town expects us to win the conference championship! And they all expect *me* to win it for them!"

His shoulders began to shake, and she saw tears in his eyes. "Staci, I can't let everybody down." He slumped on the edge of the bed, his head in his hands. "I just can't."

"It's the college scholarship, too, isn't it?" she asked softly.

Matt looked up, his eyes glistening. "You know how much that means to Mom and Dad. And I know it's my ticket to something great. If I get to go to a good school, I can be anything I want—doctor, lawyer, scientist— anything."

She had never seen him like this. She knew how much he wanted that scholarship. After all, she had cheated to try to get one herself. But she had done something wrong—and she knew it. Matt was doing something wrong, too, no matter how much he tried to deny it. Somehow, she had to make him stop.

She sat down beside him. "Matt, what if you got hold of a bad batch? I read that some people even sell steroids that were meant for animals," she said in a choking voice. "Please! It's too risky, Matt. You're the only brother I have, and I love you. I don't know what I'd do if anything ever happened to you."

"Stace, I'm fine. Nothing's going to happen to—"

Almost hysterical now, she pleaded with him. "Matt, please, please stop now." She began to cry. "For me."

He put his arm around her, and both were quiet awhile. Staci's quiet sobbing was the only sound. "Okay, you win. I'll stop now."

"Promise?" she asked through her tears.

"I promise I'll stop." He muttered something she couldn't hear.

"What did you say?"

"Nothing. I'll stop if you promise not to say anything to Mom and Dad."

She nodded. She didn't like the idea of not telling her parents. But she knew she'd do anything, promise anything just to get Matt to stop using those awful drugs.

"Oh, Matt, I'm so glad," she said through her tears of happiness and relief. "If anything happened to you..." Her voice trailed off.

Then she added, "It'll be great to have the *real* Matt Malloy back."

Eight

MATT won the next game almost single-handedly. He was like a demon on the field, rushing for nearly 300 yards, and scoring five touchdowns. It was one of the greatest performances anyone could remember. Even better, Staci heard that there were several college scouts at the game, including one from Harvard and one from Stanford!

The crowd went wild. Staci knew that she would never forget the sound of everyone in the stadium yelling, "Matt! Matt! Matt!"

Staci watched him closely. He had told her that when he tried to quit before, he had lost some of his strength. But it sure didn't look like he had lost anything. *Maybe it took several weeks after you stop using the steroids,* she thought.

During that week, she hardly saw Matt, except for the football game on Friday night.

He was getting along better with Krystal, and so he was spending a lot more time with her. And with Staci's parents so busy, she had more chores to do at home. In her spare time, she worked on her story.

One Saturday, she came home from the library. She heard Matt in his room. By all the groaning and grunting sounds, she knew that he was working out. When she was little, Matt used to bang on her door and in a gruff voice call out, "Little Pig, Little Pig, let me in." And she had a special answer.

She knocked on his door and growled, "Little Pig, Little Pig, let me in."

Matt answered, "Not by the hairs on my—" He groaned. "Chinny-chin—" Suddenly he gave a loud gasp, then groaned again.

Staci heard the heavy weight drop to the floor. "Matt?" she cried. "Are you okay?"

After a long pause, he answered in a faint voice, "Fine."

He didn't sound fine at all. "Matt!" She tried the door, but it was locked. "Let me in."

"Not by the hairs on my—" he said in a weak voice.

She banged on the door. "Let me in, or I'm calling Mom or Dad."

He slowly opened the door, then slumped down on his bed.

She stood in front of him, looking at his pale face. "Matt, what's wrong? You look awful."

"I told you I'm fine," he said, snapping at her. "I just tried to lift too much weight, that's all." He rubbed his left arm.

"You said you'd start losing your strength when you stopped using the steroids. You shouldn't be trying to lift the same weight as you did before."

"I *know* what I'm doing," he said sharply. He hunched forward and held his chest. Sweat poured down his face.

"I'm worried about you, Matt. Maybe you need to go to the doctor."

"What I *need* is for people to stop telling me what to do!" he shouted. "I'm not going to the doctor and that's final!"

Suddenly Staci knew. A chill went down her spine. "You're still on steroids, aren't you?"

"It's none of your business."

"Matt, you *promised.*"

"I said I'd quit, and I will. After the game with Hawthorne. It's only two more weeks."

Tears of frustration stung her eyes. "How can you be so stupid?! Look at you! You're sick. And you could get a whole lot sicker!"

"There's *nothing* wrong with me!" He gripped her arm so that it hurt. "Promise me

82

you won't say anything to Mom and Dad."

But Staci would not give in. "Only if you give me our old spit-in-the-hand promise that you'll absolutely stop using steroids forever after the Hawthorne game."

He looked at her for a second, then nodded. They hadn't used their special disgusting promise in ages, but they each spat on their palms, then shook hands.

She made a face and wiped her hands on her skirt. "Yuckk! Who ever thought this up?"

"You did, when you were five," Matt said. "Now, get out of here and let me work out in peace."

* * * * *

I never should have promised not to tell Mom and Dad, Staci told herself Monday. *Somebody has to make Matt come to his senses.*

After school, Staci went out to the football field to watch practice. Matt seemed all right, but the only thing she could think of was the way he had looked Saturday—pale, sweating, holding his chest.

She waited until the guys headed for the locker room. She caught up with Coach Phillips. "Coach, do you have a minute?"

He turned around, looking irritated. "Not now," he said. "Can't you see I'm busy?"

"It's about Matt."

"Who are you?"

"I'm his sister."

"Well, what about him?" Coach Phillips asked, looking at his watch.

"Uhh, well, I don't think he's feeling very well. Could you maybe let him take it easy for the next couple of weeks?"

The coach looked at her as if she'd lost her mind. "There's nothing wrong with Matt that another fifteen or twenty pounds wouldn't cure. He's not sick. He's just not strong enough. That's the problem!"

Staci could hardly believe her ears.

Then he smiled briefly and added, "Look, uh, I'll keep an eye on him, all right? But my advice is don't worry about your brother. He's as healthy as a horse."

She watched him turn and trot off to the locker room. *All he cares about is winning,* she thought, her face hot with anger. *Winning! Anything is okay as long as you're on top, number one, the winner!* she wanted to yell after him.

Then it hit her. *I'm no different from Matt. I cheated to win a scholarship. He uses illegal drugs to win football games. The only difference is that cheating on a test isn't going to hurt me—at least not physically.*

Staci needed to sit down. She wandered over to the bleachers. The thoughts raced around in her head, all jumbled. *Who am I to tell Matt not to cheat? Why should he listen to me when I've done the same thing to get an* A *on that test?* Staci put her head in her hands. She didn't know how long she had sat there, but suddenly, she had an idea. "I hope it's not too late," she whispered. Standing up, she gathered her books and headed for the school parking lot.

She stood by Mr. Knight's car. Luckily, he must have stayed a little late after football practice. When he came out, he looked surprised to see her.

"Hi, Staci. What's up? Something wrong?"

"No...well, yes."

"Get in. I'll drive you home."

He unlocked the car and held the door for her. "I saw you talking to Coach Phillips. You're not thinking of trying out for the team, are you?"

She laughed. "I wanted to talk to him about Matt, but he wouldn't listen."

"Oh?"

Now that she was in the car, she didn't know what to say. "Mr. Knight, I—" She picked at a thread on her sweater. "I have to tell you something."

"About Matt?"

She shook her head. "No. About me."

Out of the corner of her eye, she saw him nod without saying anything.

"I—uh—"

"What about you?" he asked.

"I hate to tell you. I'm too ashamed."

"This is about the last creative writing test, isn't it?"

Her head jerked up. "How—how did you know?"

"I didn't know for sure until right now," he said quietly. "Why don't you tell me about it."

Staci took a deep breath and said, "You know how I always put everything off until the last minute? Well, I hadn't gotten around to reading all the assignments." She turned and looked at him. "I didn't start out to cheat, Mr. Knight. Honest."

She explained how she had accidentally gotten into his file the first time and quickly got out again without reading the questions. "I didn't do very well on that test, and so before the last exam, I figured I'd just take a look at the first three or four questions. You know, just to give me an edge."

He stared straight ahead at the road. He wasn't going to make this any easier, she realized.

"I mean, I still had to read those assignments and answer the questions. It just saved me a lot of time. And I was careful to check for all my errors." The words she had used to justify cheating to herself sounded hollow when she said them out loud to the teacher.

"I'm sorry. I know it was wrong." She gave him a pleading look. "Will this ruin my chances for the scholarship?"

He pulled up in front of her house and turned the engine off. Then he said, "I don't know yet."

They sat there for a minute without speaking. Finally, she said, "I guess you're pretty disappointed in me."

"What do you think, Staci? With your talent and intelligence, you don't need to cheat."

She stared at her hands, wishing she could turn back the clock. "What are you going to do? Give me detention? Tell my parents?"

"I don't know that yet either, Staci," he said. "I knew someone had been in the file the Saturday before the test."

"How? I didn't touch it. I just looked at it."

"The date on the backup file had changed from the last time I had worked on the test," he explained. "I guess I didn't notice the other time."

"I'm really sorry, Mr. Knight," Staci said

softly. "I'll never cheat again. That's for sure."

"You'll find out cheating only hurts the one who cheats."

As she started to get out of the car, he added, "Staci, all Coach Phillips can think about right now is winning the conference championship. Do you want to talk to me about Matt?"

Staci paused, wondering whether she should say anything. "Well, I am kind of worried about him," she admitted.

"Worried, how?"

"Umm, I don't think he's feeling very well," she said, not wanting to say too much. "I just asked Coach if he'd let Matt take it easy the next week or so. That's all."

Mr. Knight laughed. "I can imagine his reaction to that."

Staci shot him a quick look of confusion. Even though he was the assistant coach, maybe he wasn't so gung ho on winning. Maybe she could trust him. Maybe she could tell him about Matt using steroids. He might be able to get Matt to see a doctor.

Could she betray Matt's confidence? She promised she would not tell her mom and dad. But she *didn't* promise she would not tell someone else, though.

Oh, Matt, what should I do?

When she didn't say anything, Mr. Knight said, "I've noticed a change in Matt."

"How, uh, how do you mean? He said he had a checkup."

"I'm not talking about his health now. I'm talking about his attitude. He's gotten as aggressive as a pit bull."

"I guess that's what Coach wants," Staci said.

"Matt's on steroids, isn't he?" Mr. Knight asked bluntly.

"I-I don't know what you're talking about," she said, avoiding his eyes.

"I think you know exactly what I'm talking about, Staci. He shows all the signs of a user. Quick weight and muscle growth. Acne. Hostility. Personality change. Haven't your parents noticed the change?"

"I don't think so," she said, realizing she had just about admitted that she knew Matt was on steroids. "They're both so busy with the new business."

"They should be told."

"No. Please," she begged. "I promised him I wouldn't tell them. He said he'd quit right after the Hawthorne game."

"That's not so easy to do. If we win the conference championship, then he'll want to keep strong for the play-offs."

She nodded. "I know. He said he had tried to quit, and he started losing the muscle he'd built up." She turned to him. "Mr. Knight, I'm really worried about him. I read some books on steroids, and it tells about all the terrible things that can happen."

"Tell you what. I'll talk to Matt and Coach Phillips."

"No! You can't! Don't say anything to the coach. Matt could lose any chance of getting a college scholarship."

"Don't worry," Mr. Knight said. "I don't like the idea of ruining a kid's life by turning him in. So first, I'd like to try to get him to quit on his own."

Staci felt so relieved that she almost started to cry. "I—I don't know what to say, Mr. Knight. I wouldn't think you'd want to help either Matt or me."

"Even good kids make bad decisions. All of us place too much emphasis on winning."

It was almost what she'd thought earlier.

As she climbed out of the car, he said, "Matt's lucky to have you for a sister. You cared enough to want to help him."

Lying in bed that night, she still felt as if she'd betrayed Matt, but Mr. Knight's words had helped.

Matt's lucky to have you for a sister.

Nine

T HE next afternoon, Staci waited for Deneen to leave school. They hadn't talked for the week after the test. "Mind if I walk with you?" Staci asked.

Deneen shrugged. "It's a free country."

Neither spoke for a long time. Finally, Staci adjusted her book bag, cleared her throat, and dove into the conversation headfirst. "I know you've been ticked off at me because I cheated on the test."

Deneen started to say something. But Staci held up her hand. "No, let me finish. I just wanted you to know that yesterday I told Mr. Knight what I did."

"Honest? You really told him?"

Staci nodded.

"Boy, that must have been rough. What's he going to do about it?"

"I don't know yet. I sure don't want Mom

and Dad to know. And if he knocks my grade down, I'll never get to apply to the Academy. I think I'm dead."

They stopped in front of Staci's house. "Want to come in awhile?" Staci asked.

"Can't. I have to practice. Staci, whatever happens, I'm glad you told Mr. Knight. Are you sorry you told him?" Deneen asked.

"No, not re—"

"Staci!" a booming voice shouted.

Matt stood on the front porch, his arms folded across his chest. His eyebrows were pulled down in a frown to match the rest of his angry face.

"Uh-oh, Matt looks like he could bite a log in two," Deneen whispered. "I think this is the time for me to make a quick exit. Call me later," she said with a wave.

Staci climbed the steps and faced Matt. "What's up?"

He jerked his head toward the door. "Get inside!" he shouted.

"What's the matter with you?"

He slammed the door shut. "You know what's the matter. You promised you'd keep your mouth shut about me. I thought I could trust my own sister."

"If you're talking about steroids," Staci said, "I promised I wouldn't tell Mom and Dad. I didn't tell them."

"Well, you blabbed to Knight. He cornered me today. Said he knew I was using."

"I didn't have to tell him, Matt. He'd already guessed."

Matt eyed her suspiciously. "Are you sure?"

"Yes, he said you had all the signs. He thinks Mom and Dad should know, but I asked him not to say anything to them. I told him you had promised to quit as soon as we play Hawthorne."

Staci headed for the kitchen and dumped her book bag on the table. "So, what's Mr. Knight going to do about it?" she asked Matt when he followed her.

"He wouldn't tell me. He's just going to let me sweat awhile, I guess."

That seemed to be Mr. Knight's style, she thought—to give you plenty of time to imagine the worst. "Matt, you'll probably be mad, but I told Coach Phillips that I didn't think you felt too well."

"You did *what!*" Matt exploded.

"I just asked him if you could take it easy."

Matt slammed his fist on the kitchen table, then slumped into a chair with a groan. "No wonder Coach was giving me these weird looks! He asked me if I was taking my 'vitamins.' Said I'd better be okay, or we could forget a championship for the team *and* a scholarship for me."

Matt had sounded sarcastic when he had said the word *vitamins*, Staci thought. "Coach Phillips knows you've been taking steroids, doesn't he?" she asked slowly.

"He must know," Matt answered with a laugh. "But he pretends that he's against the team using them. He puts up these little anti-drug signs in the locker room. But I've heard that his job is on the line. If we don't win the conference championship this year, he's out."

"Mr. Knight sounded as if he was really against them," Staci said.

"Sure, but he's only the assistant coach. He doesn't have any clout. If he goes to Phillips, Coach won't even listen. Because if he listens, he has to do something about it. No way will he jeopardize our chances to win."

"Well, it's only ten more days until the Hawthorne game," Staci said. "Then we won't have to worry about it anymore." She put her arm around Matt's shoulders and gave him a quick hug. "Did I ever tell you that you're my favorite brother?"

* * * * * * *

For the week before the Hawthorne game,

the entire town of Rancho Grande was in a state of hysteria. Both teams were undefeated, and the game would decide the championship and which team would go to the state play-offs. Not since the Great Mongo graduated had the high school team done so well. And everybody in town knew that most of the success was due to Matt.

The night of the game, nobody could eat a bite, which was convenient. Staci's mother was so excited, she burned the casserole.

Before Matt left for the game, Staci drew him aside. "Can I talk to you for a minute?"

"I don't have much time—but okay." He followed her into her room and leaned against the door. "You're not going to give me a big lecture about being careful, are you?"

She shook her head. "No, I just want you to know how proud I am of you."

"For what?" he asked with a wink. "My great physique, my good looks, or my brain?"

"No. I'm proud of you because, after this game, you'll be giving up the steroids."

"For Pete's sake, keep your voice down!" he said. "The walls in this house are made of tissue paper."

"Matt, I know it's going to be hard, but I just want you to know, I'm behind you one hundred percent."

"Staci, uhh, I've been meaning to talk to you about that. See, if we win tonight, that means we might go to the play-offs. I can't let everybody down. Right or wrong, this whole town has made me the big hero, comparing me to Grandpa. Do you know what a load that is? They're all depending on me to win."

That was exactly what Mr. Knight had predicted would happen. Staci's heart sank. "Matt, you promised!" she cried.

"I promise I'll cut down the dosage. I'll just take enough to—"

"If you don't stop right now, I'm going to tell Mom and Dad!"

His face hardened. "Don't threaten me, Staci."

She ran to him and threw her arms around him. "Please, let's not fight," she begged. "Not tonight." She leaned her head against his chest, and felt that his heart was beating wildly. "We won't talk about it now. You shouldn't get upset before the game."

He stroked her hair. "I love you, little sister. You're a major pain in the wazoo, but I love you."

"Matt," she said softly, "I don't care if we win or lose tonight. You're more important than any old game." She gave him a little smile. "I wasn't going to say this, but...be

96

careful. Okay?"

"I'm always careful." He flexed his muscles. "I'm Matt the Magnificent." "At least that's what Krystal says." Then he growled, "Matt, the Man-eating Tiger."

"I think you mean Matt the Modest," she said, giving him a little poke in the chest. "I love you, too, big brother." She gave him another poke, and he pretended she had really hurt him.

"Hey, take it easy!" he said with a laugh.

"Go get those bums from Hawthorne. I'll see you after the game."

* * * * * *

The Malloys, the Cusiks, the Wagners, and Krystal all sat together at the game. Everyone huddled under umbrellas, but even the rain couldn't dampen the crowd's enthusiasm. A storm had come in from the ocean, and a downpour had turned the field into a muddy mess.

"I'm glad I'm not in the band," Deneen said. "Can you imagine marching around in that mud at half time?"

"The quarterbacks won't be doing much passing tonight," Mr. Wagner said. "That ball will be as slippery as a live fish."

"Matt ought to shine," Mr. Cusik pointed out. "He'll be carrying the ball even more than usual."

"But Hawthorne's got the number one defense in the whole state," added Staci's mother. "It's going to be an all out war there tonight."

Rick, Deneen, and Staci grinned at each other. Rick whispered, "Our parents are more fanatical about the game than any of us kids."

"All except your brother." Staci nodded toward Bobby. "The game hasn't even started, and Bobby's already jumping up and down."

Rick smiled. "I think he wishes he could trade brothers with you. He thinks Matt is the greatest thing since video games. He even had his hair cut like Matt's."

The game started slowly. Both teams seemed to be feeling out not only the opponent, but the footing as well. As Deneen's dad had said, Matt carried the ball through most of the first half. Even though it was obvious that Matt was using every ounce of energy, he was held to only a few yards per carry by Hawthorne's tough defense. At the end of the first half, neither team had scored. So far, the college scouts who were at the game hadn't seen much to write home about.

The second half see-sawed back and forth.

First one team would score, then the other would come back. With only two minutes left to play in the game, the score was tied 10-10. Rancho Grande had the ball on Hawthorne's 40-yard line. The quarterback flipped the ball to Matt. He sidestepped a Hawthorne player and went wide, with players slipping and sprawling in the mud behind him. He broke several tackles and, using his head like a battering ram, drove forward to the 15-yard line for a first down. It was Matt's best run of the entire game.

The crowd was in a frenzy now. Even Krystal was screaming and stomping her feet. They felt that Rancho Grande was driving for the winning score—the score that would end the greatest season the team had ever had!

The quarterback faked a pass, which didn't fool anyone, and handed off the ball to Matt. The entire Hawthorne defense was keyed on Matt. As if she were watching in slow motion, Staci saw the Hawthorne players converge on Matt. After carrying a few players for several yards, Matt went down under a pile of bodies close to the goal line.

One by one, the muddy players scrambled to their feet. One figure still lay face down in the mud. Under the lights, it was impossible to tell who it was.

Everyone in the stands stood up, their eyes fastened on the still figure. Some of the players who had gathered around him were waving wildly to the sidelines. Something was desperately wrong, Staci thought. The trainer and a doctor ran out onto the field and knelt beside the player. A chill of fear went down Staci's back. She couldn't see Matt's number among the players standing.

The loudspeaker crackled. Staci stood stiff, not daring to breathe.

"The injured player is Rancho Grande's number twenty-eight."

Matt!

Dazed and frightened, Staci and her parents made their way to the sidelines, but were held back from getting too close. Some of the people attending to Matt were frantically trying to remove his helmet, jersey and shoulder pads.

In moments, paramedics arrived and administered CPR. A hand grasped Staci's arm. She turned to see Krystal's stricken face.

"Dear God, what has happened to Matt?" Krystal said.

The two of them clung together as they watched the paramedics transfer Matt to a gurney and wheel him to the ambulance by the gate.

Ten

STACI'S mother and father held her close as they watched the paramedics work on Matt. Even with the flashing lights of the emergency vehicles, his skin looked bluish-gray. He was so still. He was stripped to the waist, and had wires and electrodes on his chest. She had seen doctors on TV use the paddle-like instruments on patients whose hearts had stopped.

But why are they using those things? she wondered. *Matt couldn't have had a heart attack. He is too young.*

When Matt's body jerked from the shock, Staci shuddered and hid her face against her mother's shoulder. She could hear the sounds of the crowd floating across the field from the stands. Only vaguely, she realized that others had gathered around them—Mr. Knight, Rick and Deneen and their families.

After a few shocks to start the heart, the medics tried to start Matt's breathing. When he finally began to breathe on his own, Staci nearly collapsed with relief. Her legs felt as if they couldn't hold her up.

"Is—is he going to be all right?" her mother asked the medics.

"He's stabilized for the moment," one of the men said. "We're taking him to the emergency room."

On the short drive to the hospital, nobody spoke. Krystal sat beside Staci in the back seat. The two clutched each other, and for the first time, Staci realized that Krystal really did care for Matt.

At the hospital, they rushed into the emergency waiting room. At first, only a few people were there. But after awhile, Matt's teammates arrived and crowded into the room, all wanting to know if Matt was all right. Then it seemed as if half the people in town tried to push their way in.

Mr. Knight took control and herded everyone but Matt's closest friends and teammates out to the parking lot. When Staci saw Coach Phillips making his way toward them, anger swept over her. If the coach had only listened and benched Matt, he might not be in an emergency room fighting for his life. As the coach passed the players, he gave each one a pat on the back.

He came up to her father. "How's Matt?" he asked. "They told me he was doing okay."

"We don't know yet," her father said. "We're waiting for the doctor."

"Well, try not to worry," the coach answered. "Matt's as strong as a horse."

What does he know? Staci thought.

"You should see the parking lot," the coach said. "Everybody in town is out there waiting to hear how Matt's doing."

Her father nodded. "I—I guess I didn't realize just how popular Matt is."

"He's the town hero," the coach said. "When we found out that Matt was stabilized, we went on with the game. I wanted to tell Matt that we won."

"I don't think this is the time to talk about the game," Mr. Knight said quietly to Coach Phillips.

Just then, a doctor came into the waiting room and asked, "Is the family of Matt Malloy here?" The crowd moved aside to let Staci and her parents through to the doctor. "I'm Dr. Morgan. Please, follow me," he said. Staci's family followed him down the long hallway.

"How is he?" her mother cried. "I want to see him."

"Matt suffered cardiac arrest, but he has stabilized now," the doctor said in a reassuring tone of voice. "He's getting the proper medication, and his heart is back to a normal rhythm."

For the first time since she saw Matt lying on the field, Staci's own heart stopped racing, and her breathing slowed.

"I—I don't understand," her mother said. "Matt's so young. He takes care of himself. How could he possibly have a heart attack?"

"We don't have the answer yet, Mrs. Malloy," the doctor answered. "We do know his heart is enlarged. It may be a congenital condition. We've called in a heart specialist. He'll be able to tell you more after he's had a chance to examine your son."

"Can we see him now?" her father asked.

"We're taking Matt up to the coronary care unit. You can can wait up there. He'll be in bed four."

The waiting room on the third floor was empty. Her father paced up and down the corridor. Her mother sat, hands clasped, eyes closed, as if she were praying.

Coach Phillips was right, Staci thought. *Matt is as strong as a horse. Doctor Morgan said he was stabilized, and his heart was beating normally. So why am I scared?* She shivered, suddenly very cold.

Every sound she heard seemed abnormally loud—the click of hurried footsteps on the tile floors, a siren coming closer and closer, then abruptly shutting off, the murmur of voices at the nurse's station.

"When can we see our son?"

Her father's voice speaking to a nurse startled Staci. She couldn't hear the nurse's answer. Her father came back to the waiting area and took her mother's hand. "The specialist is with Matt now," he explained softly. His voice sounded strained, tired. "They're doing tests. It shouldn't be too long now."

Her mother stood up and walked to the window. "I wish it would stop raining. I *hate* rain." She swung around and her face was pinched, as if she were in pain. Her lipstick was stark against her pale face. "Maybe I shouldn't have encouraged him to play football," she said. "Why wasn't I against it like so many other mothers?"

"Honey, Matt will be fine," Staci's father said. "How about some coffee or a soda? Staci?"

Staci shook her head. Although her mouth was dry, the thought of eating or drinking anything nauseated her. She picked up a newspaper from the table. It was open to the sports section.

RANCHO GRANDE TAKES ON
ARCHRIVAL HAWTHORNE

Star running back Matt Malloy, grandson of the legendary Great Mongo Malloy, is expected to follow in his grandfather's footsteps and carry Rancho Grande to the conference championship for the first time in...

Staci dropped the paper on the table. *No wonder Matt felt that he had to use steroids. Why did people put so much pressure on him? It just wasn't fair.*

Suddenly Staci had a thought that made her blood freeze. *Had the steroids caused the heart attack? Had that time in Matt's room when he had the chest pains been a warning?*

She jumped up and headed toward the nurse's desk. She should tell the doctor. Maybe if he knew about the steroids, he'd know how to help Matt!

But as she neared the desk, her footsteps slowed. If she told anyone, Matt would no longer be a hero. He'd lose his chance for the scholarship. The whole town would turn against him.

Her fingernails dug into her palms. *What should I do? What should I do?*

Suddenly, she heard over the loudspeaker, "Code blue. Bed four. Coronary care unit."

Staci stood paralyzed. A code blue meant an emergency. Bed four was Matt's bed. She stared in disbelief as doctors and nurses rushed to the room where Matt was. A hand gripped her arm, and she realized her parents were standing beside her.

"Daddy, what's happening?" she cried. She wanted to run to Matt. She wanted to beg him not to die.

"It's going to be all right, honey. It's going to be all right." Her father kept repeating the words, as if he could convince himself.

Ice settled around Staci's heart. *Matt, don't leave us! Fight harder!* cried a voice inside her head. Unaware of anyone else, she held out her hand to Matt. *Hold on, Matt. Don't go, Matt!*

But she heard another voice in her head that said it was too late.

"No-o-o-o!" she wailed. She didn't know why, but somehow she knew it was true.

"Staci, it's going to be all—" her mother began.

"He's gone," Staci whispered. The ice around her heart spread through her body, and she shivered uncontrollably. "He's gone."

Then, as if in a trance, Staci walked slowly toward the door of the coronary care unit. People started coming out. A man in a white lab coat, rumpled shirt and crooked tie came toward them, and from the defeated look on his face, she knew that she was right.

"I'm Dr. Sullivan, the cardiologist. Please come with me," he said to the Malloys.

She glanced at her mother's and father's grief-stricken faces. *They know, too,* she thought. Silently, they followed the doctor to a quiet room.

"Please sit down," Dr. Sullivan said gently.

"Matt?" Her mother's voice trembled as she spoke.

The doctor pulled up a chair. His face looked strained and tired. "Matt had another heart attack. We were able to control the severe irregularity the first time, but there was too much damage. Matt is dead. I'm very sorry."

"Oh, God," Staci's mother whispered. "No. No." She kept shaking her head. "No!" She burst into tears. Her father held her mother. He kept biting his lips and swallowing hard, trying to keep back his own tears.

Staci sat numb, unable to cry. Her eyes felt hot and dry. Her head seemed to explode with the words, *Matt is dead...Matt is dead...Matt is dead.*

When her mother's sobbing subsided, the doctor asked if they'd like to be with Matt awhile. Staci's arms hung heavily at her sides.

She felt outside of herself. Part of her watched the scene from a distance, and the other part tried to push the pain away.

"I'll go find Krystal and see if she wants to say goodbye to Matt," her father said quickly, as if he needed to get away by himself.

Staci's mother took her hand, and together they went in to see Matt. Her mother sobbed and fell to her knees beside the bed. She caressed Matt's face and stroked his hair.

Staci could hardly bear her mother's anguish. She stood back, staring at Matt. Now her senses seemed too sharp. Every sound echoed in her ears. Every detail was carved in her mind, and she knew she'd remember this moment, remember the pain, feel the pain, for as long as she lived.

Matt looked so pale. His fingernails were dirty. Mud. The game. Matt had been struggling to get to the goal line, to score the winning touchdown. It seemed like a lifetime ago—and it was. Matt's lifetime.

Her father came into the room. He was alone. It must have been too hard for Krystal to tell Matt goodbye. Her father drew aside the curtain around the bed, and she watched her parents say their goodbyes. She knew that they didn't mean to exclude her, but she felt alone. Her father gave a great, shuddering sigh and lifted her mother to her feet. "We'd better go now," he said softly.

"Daddy, let me be alone with Matt—just for a minute," Staci whispered.

He nodded. "We'll be outside."

When the door closed behind her parents, Staci took Matt's hand and held it in her own. "I wish the doctor would have let me be in here with you—before...Maybe I could have kept you—"

Her voice broke and, for the first time, tears slid down her cheeks. "Oh, Matt, nothing will ever be the same without you. I'll miss you so much."

She tried to smile, but it hurt too much. "Did I ever t-tell you that you're my favorite broth—" The words caught in her throat.

"Goodbye, big brother. I love you."

Eleven

W HEN they returned from the hospital,
the house seemed strange—cold and un-
familiar—as if it belonged to some other
family.

She watched her father walk through the
quiet, empty house. His shoulders were
stooped, and suddenly, he looked like an old
man. Staci knew their family would never be
the same again. Nothing would ever be the
same again.

Staci wandered into her bedroom. She
looked at the gifts that Matt had given to her
over the years—a teddy bear, porcelain figu-
rines, his old skates, a wooden box he had
made, his first football, which he autographed
for her, *TO MY BEST PAL.*

Football! Bobby's football. As usual, she
had put off asking Matt to sign it. Now it was
too late. She stared at the words, *TO MY*

BEST PAL. The football looked almost like Bobby's. Maybe he wouldn't realize that it wasn't his. She looked at all the other gifts Matt had given her. She'd give this one to Bobby.

"Matt, I hope you don't mind," she whispered. "You're Bobby's hero."

Staci heard scratching sounds outside her door in the hall. When she stepped out of her room, she saw Hal sitting in front of Matt's door, pawing it and whining as if begging Matt to let him in.

"Oh, Hal," she said, dropping to her knees by the dog, who was looking at her with his big, dark eyes. She buried her face in his golden coat. "Matt won't be coming home any—more," she said. "We're both—going to miss—him."

She felt stiff and awkward as she got to her feet. She looked at Matt's closed door. He didn't like anyone to come in without permission. But she knew he wouldn't mind now.

Her hand shook as she turned the knob. Still whining softly, Hal followed her inside. She switched on the bedside light and looked around. Matt's weights and exercise equipment, his telescope, the banners and posters on the walls, his games and books—all were there waiting for him to return. It seemed so unreal that he'd never be coming back.

His blue turtleneck sweater and old jeans were on the bed. She pushed them aside and stretched out. Hal jumped up on the bed and lay next to her. "What are we going to do without him, Hal?" she whispered.

She looked up at the sky painted on the ceiling. She stared at the planets that Matt had so carefully drawn. She could almost feel Matt's presence, as if he were close by, and slowly the tenseness left her body.

She picked up a picture of Matt and her from the bedside table. It was taken when he was fifteen and she was eleven. He looked so skinny and frail. No one would have ever believed he would turn out to be a star football player.

She sat up suddenly, startling Hal, who gave a sharp bark. Ignoring him, she jumped up and crossed to the desk where Matt had kept his "aspirin."

She picked up the bottle, trying to make up her mind whether or not to flush the horrible things down the toilet and be rid of them forever. Or should she tell her parents? Matt was gone. Surely her promise not to tell didn't mean anything anymore. Staci stood holding the bottle, unable to decide what was the best thing to do.

"I—I can't decide," she whispered. "I'll wait until the morning, when I've had a little sleep. Mom and Dad have enough pain now."

Staci didn't sleep well that night. And during the hours when she wasn't lying awake, staring at the ceiling and crying softly, she had strange dreams. When the morning light finally peeped in behind the curtains, she rubbed her burning eyes and slowly got up. She thought she knew what she should do.

When she went to get breakfast, she found her father sitting alone in the kitchen. "I see you didn't get much sleep last night either," he said.

"Dad, there's something I have to tell you." Before she could change her mind, she held out the bottle of pills.

"What are these?" he asked.

"Steroids," she answered. "These are anabolic steroids."

"Steroids?" Her dad shook his head. "I don't understand."

Taking a deep breath, Staci began to explain. Her voice was weak to begin with, but grew stronger as she continued. "They're Matt's. He felt he needed to take them to be big and strong. He thought everyone in town was depending on him. He was trying to be as good as the Great Mongo. He just wanted you

114

and Mom and everybody to be proud of him. And he didn't want to let anybody down."

A flash of terrible pain crossed her father's face, and he closed his eyes.

"Daddy, I tried to get him to stop. He promised he would. I'm sorry, I'm sorry. I never should have promised not to tell you. Maybe he'd—he'd still be alive."

"No, no, don't even think like that, honey," her father said. "No matter what caused Matt's death, it's not your fault. If anyone's to blame, it's your mother and I. If only we hadn't been so busy..."

Both sat quietly for a time.

"Does anyone else know?" her father asked.

"Rick and Mr. Knight suspected it. Matt told me that Coach Phillips knew."

"He knew and didn't do anything?" he asked sharply. "He's got some explaining to do." Then he gave her a hug. "I'm glad you told me, honey. I know this has been rough on you. You did the right thing."

Staci nodded. It was strange, but in a way, she felt as if one of Matt's heavy weights had been lifted off her. She didn't feel quite so alone now.

* * * * *

As they stepped inside the funeral home on Monday, Staci wished with all her heart that she could have stayed home. "Why do we have to have a funeral anyhow? Matt's not here. He won't know the difference."

"Funerals are for the people left behind," her mother said softly. "It's hard to start a new life until there is a final note to the old."

Hesitantly, Staci went into the large viewing room. Her heart pounded as she walked slowly over to the casket. She kept her head turned away. She was afraid he might look different and she wouldn't even recognize him.

As if she understood, her mother put her arm around Staci. "It's all right."

Slowly, Staci let her eyes rest on Matt. He was wearing his letter jacket. He looked as if he were taking a nap. "Matt," she whispered, "maybe now you can see the stars close up."

At one o'clock, Matt's friends, the football team and most of the students in his class came to say goodbye. Rick, Deneen and Krystal stood by Staci's side as she nodded to each one. Everyone was crying, even the big, strong football players. She realized then that her mother was right. They all needed to say one last goodbye to Matt.

Only a few people were told about Matt using steroids—family members, the

Wagners, the Cusiks, Krystal and Coach Phillips. While everyone was sad about Matt's death, Staci was surprised about how differently some people had reacted to him using steroids.

She remembered Krystal, with tears rolling down her cheeks, telling her, "It's my fault. I called him Matt the Magnificent. I always oohed and ahhed about his muscles. I should have told him that he didn't need to impress me with his big muscles. Didn't he know I loved him, no matter what he looked like or how popular or important he was?"

"He knew you loved him," Staci had told Krystal. "He knew."

Then Staci recalled the evening when Coach Phillips came by to return Matt's things from the locker room, and her father confronted him.

"The doctor said that Matt had an enlarged heart, hypertension, and cardiac dysrhythmia. We got the autopsy report today. The coroner thinks that steroids were a contributing factor to his death," her father had said.

"Look, I'm as sorry as anybody about your boy, Ed. But I didn't know about him being on steroids," Coach Phillips had said.

"I think you do," her father had said coldly. "Matt told Staci that several players were using and that you looked the other way."

Coach Phillips seemed to pass off any responsibility. "So maybe a few kids use them once in a while. They feel that they need that extra edge. My players want to win so badly. There's no way I could stop them from doing whatever it takes. Believe me, all the other teams use them. Steroids are everywhere. And we have to be competitive to win."

"So you're willing to risk the kids' lives to win football games?" her father had said to him.

"Hey, every time a kid steps on the football field, he's taking a risk. It's a rough sport— and the kids know it. That's why they want to be as tough as they can be," Coach Phillips had said.

He seemed very nervous that her father might go public with the information.

"Just think what you'll do to Matt's reputation," the coach had said. "He's a big hero in town, just like your pop was. It's too late to save his life, but you *can* save his good name."

When her father didn't respond, the coach went on. "It was just a one-in-a-million chance that the steroids would do him any harm."

"Even if it is rare for a boy to die," her father had said, "it's your responsibility to watch these kids. You should have been able to tell that Matt was using steroids."

"What about you? Your wife's an athlete. How come you two didn't see it?"

Staci's dad had looked as if he had been struck. He answered in a weak voice. "I don't need you to tell me that we're responsible, too. We have to live with that the rest of our lives."

"Look, just think about what I've said," the coach had said as he stood up to leave. "Why not keep it quiet? What *good* will it do to bring it all up now?"

That phrase now echoed in Staci's mind. *What good will it do.*

It was almost two o'clock and time to get ready to go to the cemetery, when Bobby came in with several of his friends. He was proudly carrying the autographed football she had given him.

Bobby took his friends over to the casket. "I'm going to be just like Matt," he said. "My brother told me Matt used to be little and skinny like me. If he can get big and strong, so can I."

Staci wanted to scream out, *No, Bobby, you don't want to be like Matt!*

Bobby turned to Staci's mother. "Mrs. Malloy, do you think it would be okay if I gave my football to Matt? He might need one where

119

he is now."

Staci's eyes stung. She saw tears well up in her parents' eyes.

"Bobby," Rick said sharply, "you can't ask a thing like that."

"It's all right," Mrs. Malloy whispered. She ruffled Bobby's hair. "But are you sure, Bobby?"

Bobby hesitated a moment, looked at the ball, then at the casket. "I think Matt might need it."

Staci's father gently laid the football beside Matt. Staci reached over and turned it so that the words were showing: *TO MY BEST PAL*.

"Staci," her mother said softly, "It's time to go to the cemetery."

"I'd like to say one last goodbye," she answered. "I have to tell Matt one more thing."

When her mother walked away, Staci knelt beside the casket. The scent of all the flowers around the casket was overpowering.

"Matt, I hope you understand why I had to tell Mom and Dad about the steroids," She looked up to see her parents arm in arm waiting for her. "I have to go now." The lump in her throat choked her, and she whispered, "Goodbye, big brother."

* * * * *

A few days after the funeral, Mr. Knight told Staci that she wasn't going to be able to apply for the scholarship. Her grades weren't good enough. Staci felt oddly empty, but not devastated.

"I guess it's my own fault," she said with a sigh, standing by Mr. Knight's desk after school.

When you've just lost a brother, losing out on a chance to go to a summer academy doesn't seem very important.

"Well, I guess I better get home," she said.

But at the door she hesitated.

"Is there something wrong?" Mr. Knight asked.

"I told my mom and dad about Matt using steroids," Staci said looking down at the ground. "I—I just keep thinking that somebody should do something more, before anyone else is hurt."

Mr. Knight looked at her. "Doing something more is a decision you and your parents have to make, Staci," he said slowly. "You have to do what you think is right."

* * * * *

That night, Staci told her parents about not getting to apply for the scholarship.

"I didn't really feel like going anyway," she said. "Not after everything."

But there was something else on Staci's mind as the family ate dinner quietly.

"Mom, Dad, I was wondering if you've decided if we should tell the truth about Matt."

Her parents looked at each other. Her dad said, "Well, we've been so busy with the shop that we haven't had much of a chance to think about what might be the best way." Her mother nodded her agreement.

"The reason I asked is that I'm trying to write a story about Matt and the steroids. I sort of gave up on my Halloween story. It didn't seem very—important anymore. I was wondering if maybe I should send my story to the newspaper."

Mr. Malloy didn't say anything. It made Staci wonder if she had said the wrong thing by bringing the subject up. Her parents still wanted to let people know, didn't they?

"Oh, Staci," her mother said sadly. "We do want to tell people. It's just that we want to do it the best way. We want to wait for the right time."

"Let us think about it a little more, honey," her dad said.

"Okay," Staci said. *But when,* she wondered, *would be the right time to tell people something like this?*

"By the way," her dad said, "the principal of the high school called to say they're going to have an assembly on Friday to honor Matt. The team wanted to dedicate the conference trophy to Matt. Reporters and TV people will be there. Some of the team members will be giving short speeches, and he wanted to know if you'd say something about Matt."

"I don't know. I guess I could," Staci said.

* * * * *

On the afternoon of the dedication, Staci felt nervous. The large auditorium was full of students and adults. She noticed newspaper reporters and a TV cameraman setting up his equipment. They made her even more nervous.

Two members of the senior class escorted her parents to front row seats. They told Staci to join some of the team members up on the stage. From the stage, Staci saw Rick's parents with Bobby in the third row. *It's nice that they could be here,* she thought.

Mr. Gassner, the principal, spoke first, saying how proud they all were of Matt. He held up the trophy. "Without Matt Malloy, our school would never have won the conference championship. He was—and is—the inspiration for the entire football team."

Next, the co-captain of the team stood at the microphone. "The guys have lost a good friend," he said. His voice was rough, as if he were trying not to cry. "Matt Malloy was the greatest. We're going miss him."

Coach Phillips, looking sad, took the mike next. "Matt Malloy was everything a coach could ask for," he said. "Nobody worked harder or gave more of himself to his teammates, his school, his town. He was a true hero in every sense."

As he turned the microphone over to Staci, his words rang in Staci's ears. *A true hero in every sense.*

She glanced at Bobby in the third row. *How many kids like Bobby are there in this town,* she wondered, *kids who thought my brother was the greatest?*

What was it Bobby had said at the funeral home, when he gave the football back to Matt? *I'm going to be just like Matt. If he can get big and strong, so can I.*

The principal cleared his throat, and Staci realized the people were waiting for her to speak. Staci looked at Coach Phillips. The question he had asked in their living room came back to her. *What good will it do to bring it all up now?*

Then she glanced over at Mr. Knight, sitting with the team. He smiled at her. He had said that she had to do what she thought was right.

She straightened her shoulders and said, "My brother was a hero all right, but not the way Coach Phillips means. Matt was a wonderful human being. But a human being with faults just like everyone else."

The room was absolutely silent.

She took a deep breath. *Matt, I hope you understand.*

"My brother was using steroids."

She heard loud gasps. She looked at her parents, who nodded at her. Staci saw that they were holding hands.

She went right on. "Matt wanted to have an edge, to be bigger and stronger, to help the team, to make everybody proud. So he used steroids."

A flash from a camera blinded her for a second. "Matt didn't think they could hurt him," she said. "He might be alive now if he hadn't used them. He fooled himself. Matt made a wrong choice and—and—he paid for it. But knowing my brother, I don't think he'd

125

want other kids to take a chance with their lives."

She looked at the team members. "I know some of you feel betrayed. But my family and I feel betrayed, too, by the people who sell steroids to kids, and by people—" she glanced toward the coach, "who know the risks and do nothing. And by people who look the other way and pretend it's not happening in their school. And by people who want to win so badly they'll risk anything, even kids' lives."

Every eye in the auditorium was fixed on Staci.

"I came here to give a little speech about how wonderful my brother was. Instead, I think I'll read a little bit of a story I've been trying to write about steroids."

She looked down from the podium at her parents. Her mother wiped tears from her eyes, and her father smiled and nodded again at Staci.

Staci's heart was breaking, but her voice was strong and steady. "My story," she said, "is titled *MY BROTHER IS DEAD*."

About the Author

ALIDA E. YOUNG lives with her husband in the high desert of Southern California. When she's not researching or writing a new novel, she enjoys taking long walks in the desert. To help her write her novels, she likes to put herself in the shoes of her characters, to try to feel things the way they would. Alida tries to feel the pain and hurt as well as the happiness and joy. When she's writing a book that requires research, such as *Dead Wrong*, she talks to many different experts. "Everyone is so helpful," Alida explains. "They go out of their way to help."

Other Willowisp books by Alida include *Is My Sister Dying?; Summer Cruise, Summer Love; I Never Got to Say Good-bye,* and the popular Megan the Klutz books.